THREE
LIVES

THREE
LIVES

Louis Auchincloss

HOUGHTON MIFFLIN COMPANY

Boston · New York · London

1993

Library of Congress Cataloging-in-Publication Data

Auchincloss, Louis.
Three lives / Louis Auchincloss.
p.   cm.
ISBN 0-395-65567-6
I. Title.
PS3501.U25T48   1993
813'.54—dc20   92-27588
CIP

Book design by Anne Chalmers

Printed in the United States of America

BP   10   9   8   7   6   5   4   3   2   1

FOR JOE KANON
FRIEND AND EDITOR

Contents

The Epicurean

1

I am six years older than our century, having been born in 1894 in Troy, New York, on the Hudson River, in the big plain yellow villa with the double row of French windows near the Chisolm Iron Works which Father had taken over on his father's death.

Henry Adams in his *Education*, following the useful yin and yang of Chinese philosophy, divided the essential elements of his childhood between winter and summer, Boston and Quincy, city and country. Winter was the effort to live; summer was tropical license. Boston was the unity of school; Quincy, the multiplicity of nature.

My yin and yang were my parents. Father was discipline, duty, rigor, tradition, righteousness and . . . death. Mother was beauty, pleasure, kindness and, I suppose, in her own charming way, at least to a puritan, sin.

Father, who played a strong negative role in the development of my character, was himself a partial victim of his era, a son who inherited the drive and obsessions of his sire with none of the genius. His progenitor, founder of the iron works, who emigrated from Scotland in the eighteen thirties, was a familiar type of nineteenth-century tycoon, though not of the crude "robber baron" variety. Grandfather had been a rigid Calvinist, as sternly confident of his own election to paradise as he was of the damnation of his enemies, who had built a large business out of nothing and had little to show for it but the showy mansion which custom required. In his home he had been serenely benevolent; in his office, coldly exacting. He had personified the double moral standard of his century: a high and strict one for his personal relationships, with a much wider latitude for the market-place.

Father, on the other hand, had taken nothing of the paternal religion but its darkness. He never went to church, never sought the consolation of promised bliss after death by hymn or prayer. But if he abandoned heaven he clung to hell, driven by a conscience which seemed to make the unpleasant choice always the right one.

The inner person, however, was by no means reflected in the outer. Father was what my old Scottish nurse used to call "a fine figure of a man": tall and straight with strong features in a lineless square countenance, black hair combed slickly back and dark suits which never showed a wrinkle. Furthermore, he had a relish for the good things of a material existence; his house and gardens were beautifully maintained, and his table had the finest foods and wines. Yet everything proceeded from the same inexorable sense of what his murky deity or demiurge — one that offered him neither love nor charity nor posthumous reward — expected of Augustus Chisolm.

This grim spiritual presence must have hovered particularly over the smoky heart of the Chisolm Iron Works, which spread southwards towards Albany down the east bank of the Hudson, for to Father there was no higher duty than keeping those mills and blast furnaces grinding out horseshoes. The advent of the automobile had already, when I was in my early teens, spelled the doom of the plant, but Father turned a deaf ear to the pleas of relatives and friends that he make plans for the sale or conversion of the business, insisting, with a near fanatical stubbornness, that the horseless carriage, noisy and dangerous, would merely supplement and never replace the noble steed. He even borrowed recklessly from his bank to buy out his more skeptical sisters. Nothing would persuade him that the Chisolm Iron Works were not his own grim destiny and that of his only son.

Even on vacations — and there *were* vacations (they were part of the ritual), including trips to Europe — he could be a severe trial. What may be difficult for a later generation to comprehend was how readily many of the rich of that era managed to turn seeming luxury into dust and ashes for their families. In the great restaurants of Paris and Rome, in the gilded dining saloons of giant Cunarders, we were rarely allowed to enjoy a meal, so constantly were succulent dishes snatched from under our raised forks to be sent back to the kitchen with Father's sharp and specific reproaches to the chef. And when we motored, we had to descend from the big hired Panhard or Minerva limousine at the *banlieue* of any metropolis to trudge through the streets, hot and weary in the summer heat, that we might learn to appreciate that not all of the populace enjoyed the palace hotel that was our destination. Father insisted that we always be kept on notice of the value of our privileges.

Mother was different; she lived in a sanctuary immune to her husband's injunctions. It was not she who had to descend from the Panhard or see a plate she had chosen whisked away from under her nose. But then her charm would have daunted a man stronger and more stubborn than Gus Chisolm.

How shall I describe it? She had a way of humping her shoulders and twinkling her eyes when she was pleased with something you had said, and this, followed by a radiant smile, placed you and her in the coziest kind of private relationship, which at the same time, oddly enough, did not exclude the rest of the world, with which she sought always to be on the best of terms. Her eyes were large and black and full of laughter, her eyebrows long and thick, and her brown hair was pulled straight back over her scalp with a rising curl in the middle and a Psyche knot behind. But her great feature was her lovely skin which changed subtly with her moods: a cool ivory with detachment, a glowing pink with indignation, a tint of the palest blue with love. Mother's charm operated on all the world; it was impossible not to be on good terms with her, and even her rare fits of anger, usually excited by some injustice to others, were attractive in that it was so evident that they would pass.

Father, while conceding the sanctuary in which she moved, like a goddess in a shielding cloud, struggled to limit her influence on her son and daughter, particularly on the former. Adoring her, he could still regard his adoration as a weakness and his Lorelei as a constant threat to his stout little bark of self-imposed duty. Everything about her, her charm, her beauty, her gravity-destroying gaiety, the money lavished on her by her rich and indulgent father, even the lofty morals which *appeared* to sustain her, reinforced her husband's perverse conception of her as a *femme fatale*. Had he really ever expected, by an exchange of altar vows, to bend this dryad to his will? His simple hope must have been that her generous nature would ultimately convert her to his own high sense of all that was owed to the iron works and the traditions of the Chisolms. And when that hope proved an illusion, when she still persisted in questioning, however gently but with irresistible logic, why they were bound to a dreary small-town life and a failing business when her own parent was only too happy to open for both of them the gates of Fifth Avenue, Newport and Paris, he could only consent, with whatever anguish of heart, to an arrangement whereby *she* would have the enjoyment of such oases, for as many months of the year as she desired, while he remained perched, a lonely puritan, on his Trojan rock.

To understand why Mother, with her conventional views of the duties of a loving wife, should have shown herself so unimpeded, at least geographically, by the marriage tie, the reader must meet my maternal grandfather. Eliza Chisolm was the only child of Frank Chase, who was what was then known as an international lawyer. His pose as an Old World diplomat, a wise, skeptical Metternich, the valued intimate of kings and premiers, was really the mask of a practitioner ever ready to provide his corporate clients with a jurisdiction where wrong became right. His long snowy white hair, his small plump formally clad figure, his gleaming grey eyes, haughty nose and authoritative throat-clearings, and, above all, his cheerfully arrogant stance as the polylingual master of ancient European guile, allowed him to dominate and dazzle his grubbily industrious New York partners like some gaudy peacock in a partridge pen. A widower, he spent more than half the year abroad in a showy marble mansion in the Parc Monceau crammed with huge gilded Louis XIV things where he expected his only child to act as his housekeeper and hostess for weeks at a time.

This, of course, provided Mother with the needed excuse for an escape from Troy. Grandpa never made any bones with me about his low opinion of my father, whom he described tersely as a "loser," but he was far too clever to say this to Mother, urging instead his own greater need for her services by slandering his own robust health with the claim of a fibrillating heart and even maliciously insinuating that Father, obsessed with his iron works, was really just as happy alone. But I believe Grandpa's trump card was the veiled threat that he might leave to charity at least some part of a fortune which would be wasted on a daughter too determined to lose her life and opportunities in a Yankee small town. This would have given Mother, particularly in view of her own rational doubts as to the future of the iron works, an almost moral obligation to save an inheritance for her children by doing, after all, what she wanted to do. Poor Father! I can afford to exclaim it now. He didn't have a chance against the wily progenitor of his lovely spouse.

Ah, but he could still make her pay a price, and that price was myself. Father was willing to let her take my younger sister Bella to Paris; in fact, he was willing to surrender Bella largely to the maternal control. His dark gods had little interest in the female sex; in the family women were dolls; outside the family they could be deadly sirens. But the only son had to be trained for his destiny and brought up in Troy near the iron works which he would one day manage. Paris with its time-dishonored lures was obviously out of the question for a young man, and even the New England preparatory schools, the *sine qua non* in the education of our class, were vetoed by Father, who had been sent by parents still imbued with the standards of the Old World to a Scottish public school where he had learned to his abiding horror what boys may do if closeted too long and too closely together. So an *entente*, not altogether *cordiale*, was struck between my parents: Mother would have her Gallic interludes with Bella, and I would stay home and go to high school in Troy.

I'm sure it pained Mother to leave me, but perhaps not too much. She lived so intensely in the immediate present that for someone to be absent was also to be a bit out of mind. She accepted the fact that she lived in a man's world, and no doubt considered that Father was within his rights. She may even have thought that a Spartan training was a good one for a boy. And had she spent more time in Troy, could she have made my life easier? Somewhat, perhaps, but scarcely enough to justify blighting her own.

She and Grandpa certainly made a wonderful couple. They argued and fought and roared with laughter together like two children. The big Paris house was always full of guests, and she protected Grandpa from grass widows just as easily and smoothly as he, with malice prepense towards his absent son-in-law, produced handsome and unattached males to meet her at dinner. But I don't think that Mother, for all her gentle society flirting, ever had an affair. She told me in later years that she hadn't, and I saw no reason to disbelieve her. She and I had achieved by then a near total candor. And I doubt that she ever quite fell out of love with Father — at least while he was alive. Rare is the woman who will undervalue a strong and faithful love.

Grandpa Chase enjoyed the Paris visits, rare and brief though Father stipulated they should be, of his only grandson. The old boy admired good looks, and it must be conceded that mine were that, for they play a sufficient role in my story. He took me about with him, on rides in the Bois de Boulogne, to dinners at his club and to racy plays and girlie shows. He even took care of my initiation, at the age of sixteen, into the delights of love. One morning when we were riding in the park, he asked me bluntly:

"Have you had a woman yet, Nat? I know you boys start later in the States. I didn't have my first till I was twenty. But over here we get on to it early, and I'll be glad to fix you up. All clean and neat with no complications. Just give me the word."

For a moment I was speechless. Had I really heard the old

satyr correctly? He was such an odd medley of sentimental effusions and worldly wisdom, like a merry Santa Claus stuffing a condom in my stocking. But my throat was constricted with instant hot desire. "I haven't had much experience, sir, I mean in the real thing. It isn't so easy with the girls I know in Troy."

"Helen hasn't made her appearance there yet?" He chuckled. "Well, luckily Paris is here and now. We'll find just the gal for you. And don't worry about it. Some fellows are a bit nervous the first time. She'll take everything right off your hands. You'll find it's like rolling off a log. How about tomorrow?"

"Or today if you like, sir!" I was almost bursting out of my riding pants.

He winked. "Not a word about this to your mother, you know."

But years later, when I told her about it, Mother's laugh did not sound in the least surprised.

Grandpa sent me that very afternoon to the Left Bank apartment of a lively and cheerful lady who received me as if I'd been her lover for weeks. Looking back with less dazzled eyes, I can see that she was probably well over thirty, an actress of small roles and one of the old goat's regular chicks. Never mind. I had a wonderful time and have always been grateful to Grandpa for sparing me the awkwardness that attended the introduction of so many of my contemporaries to the rites of love.

Mother sailed back to New York with me that June; it was her turn for a summer sojourn in Troy. While there she always did her best to make up to Father for her absences. She filled the house with smiles and flowers, and even he became almost human. He actually agreed to attend a picnic with champagne which she proposed to give for the boys and girls of my high school class on the bank of the river. Looking, in pink organdy, like a girl herself, she enchanted my friends, none of whom I, doubtful of the quality of the paternal reception, had ever ventured to invite to the mansion.

One friend, Alec Storrs, overrefreshed, no doubt, by the unaccustomed libation, waxed almost impertinent.

"Tell me, lovely lady," he apostrophized Mother, holding high his glass, "how one so blessed as yourself can ever desert the City of Light for our dreary burg? Or is it just the kindness of your heart that takes pity on our plight and wafts you across the ocean to our aid?"

I noted that Mother was careful not to meet Father's disapproving eye. "But, my dear young man, this is my *home!*" She extended white arms to the slowly churning Hudson. "Is there a nobler stream in all of France? I should never leave these banks were it not that a dear old parent needs my loving care abroad. Isn't it so, my dearest?" Here she blew a kiss to Father. "Alas, we cannot always do the things we want."

Storrs emitted a comic groan. "What can I do to make my old man move to Paris?" He raised his glass again. "To Lutetia!"

"Don't despair, my friend," Mother admonished him. "Remember the playwright who said that good Americans go to Paris when they die." She appeared to be struck with a thought. "Where do you suppose the bad ones go?"

"To Troy!" several shouted, and everybody laughed.

Everybody but Father, who rose and directed his butler to start repacking the family picnic hampers.

A month later, after Mother had returned to France, Father, almost shyly, asked me at the breakfast table if I would like to give another picnic for my friends. I responded dryly that it would be no fun without Mother, and I don't think I minded in the least that I might have cut him to the quick.

2

I can see now, looking back, that it was not Father's deliberate aim to make me unhappy, though it is hard to believe that he did not derive some unconscious pleasure from it. But his professed intention was to make me a gentleman and a leader worthy of carrying on the Chisolm name and managing the iron works, and to accomplish this he subjected me to myriad tests and humiliations. Everything I did, from a history learned, a poem conned, a golf or tennis stroke or even my conversation at the family board, was immediately graded and contrasted with a simultaneously created higher standard. My appearance, my clothes and my manners were constantly criticized, and even before company, if I ventured to join in the discussion at table, I was apt to be checked with a curt "I wasn't aware that anyone had asked your opinion, Nathaniel." I was like an attack dog, trained to a snarling resentment by constant blows.

When Father decided that I needed more intellectual stimulation than that supplied by our local high school before matriculating at Harvard, he arranged to have me tutored at home for my last two years. He provided an excellent teacher, a scholar from New York City who lived in our house while he worked on his doctoral thesis, and I learned more Latin and French and physics than most of my contemporaries, but the isolation from my age group and the austerity of the home atmosphere tended to make me moody and sullen, and I would occasionally break away to drink beer and carouse with my old high school friends, sometimes staying out overnight. On one such occasion Father had me sought out and returned by the police. For the first time I listened to his ranting stony-faced and refused to excuse myself. I continued to obey him after that, but there was no further pretense that my compliance was anything but submission to *force majeure*.

My physical resemblance to Father was commented on by friends and relatives, and although he was considered a very handsome man, I was conscious only of the rigidity or, to me, the woodenness of his appearance, and I tried not to emulate this, even going so far as to affect a negligent, at times an almost sloppy, air. But it was never quite successful, and I have always been a bit of a ramrod. Still, I can see that I may have struck some of my Harvard classmates as a vaguely romantic character, solitary, at times morose, seemingly eaten by an inner discontent, with the reputation of being a kind of prince in a dusky mill town whose riches might make him one day a figure in the great world. But I did not see it that way. I assumed that the young men with whom my father expected me to associate, the heirs of Beacon Street or of East Side Manhattan, would look down their noses at the son of a small-town ironmonger who had not attended a New England church school. And so I proceeded to alienate them still further by keeping aloof, by working hard (not then fashionable) and, worse, by associating with men of the least social status, many of whom had to work in laundries or restaurants to pay their tuition.

Of course, this was an obvious way to get back at Father. When he queried me about my friends, I took care to name the ones who would give him the greatest shock.

"Sidney Cohen, did you say? And his father's *what*? A

rabbi? Is *this* what I've been spending my good money for?
Haven't I told you that one of the main purposes of college
is to make friends who will be useful to you in life? An
education you can get from books and tutors. You don't go
to Harvard to mix with rabbis and cantors and God knows
what else. At least I trust you will not embarrass me by
inviting them to Troy."

As if I would ever have thought of doing so! As if I was
proud of my home! But my failure to cultivate the kind of
friends Father wanted had now another and stronger cause.
I had been captivated by a woman who would have been
anathema to any young Cabot or Lowell.

Ellen Hardy was a bookkeeper at the iron works, where
Father had made me work six weeks every summer since I
was fifteen. I had started as a manual laborer in the steamy
rolling mill, then moved on to the furnaces of the rivet fac-
tory and from there to the trickier task of loading and push-
ing balls of puddled metal in iron buggies, but by the end of
my freshman year I had graduated to the accounting department.

Ellen was the assistant to the comptroller. She was not
more than a half-dozen years my senior, but in knowledge
of the world she was easily double my age. She never, however, flaunted her capabilities. Dark and handsome, with
raven hair combed straight back to a tight knot, she had a
calm and lofty demeanor softened by eyes which seemed to
be repressing the impulse to smile at surrounding inepti-
tudes. Her dress was simple, even severe, as was the fashion
for female office workers in that day: she wore a simple white
blouse with a plain grey or brown skirt. She immediately
dazzled me.

It was not hard. I was a pushover. My relationships with
women (not counting my Paris fling and a couple of Saturday nights in the Albany red-light district) had so far been

confined to the dainty young ladies of Trojan society whose company I rarely sought. With only a handful of men friends and a barren family life, I was hideously lonely, however strongly I tried to persuade myself that mine was a prideful and voluntary solitude, and when there was added to this the sexual frustration of an eighteen-year-old in the society of that day, it is easy to see that Ellen did not have to be a siren.

Her first job was to train me to be her assistant, and she did so with patience and efficiency. She never praised or blamed: if I did a thing right it was accepted; if not, it had to be done over — that was all. I worked very hard, determined to get my brief apprenticeship over and to close the gap between teacher and pupil. I thought I had flared in her a natural resentment of the society which could allow a callow college kid to be the heir of the iron works from which she eked out so modest a living, and deemed an adroit apology for this my best way into her good graces.

I was not so forward, after my brief training period was over and I was working with her more as an equal, to invite her for dinner in town, but as we both brought sandwiches to work and as I had only a table in the file room, I asked if I might join her for lunch in her office. She could hardly refuse, and this soon became a habit.

She was not a native, and I found I could amuse her with stories of our town. She became almost friendly, though she always retained a certain reserve and a certain mild sarcasm of manner. Whether it was because I was the boss's son, or her office inferior, or simply a fresh younger man who might get "ideas," I could not tell. It might have been all of these. But it was obvious that she wouldn't have put up with me at all had she disliked me. At last the day came when I risked a direct challenge.

"What do you think I'm thinking when I look at all this?"

Here I gestured toward the window which framed the smoking chimneys of the mills. "That I'm crowing to myself: 'One day I'll own it all! And then I can say to this man: come, and he cometh, and to that man: go, and he goeth'?"

Ellen smiled. "*Is* that what you'll say?"

"What do *you* say?"

"What makes you think I think about you at all?"

"Oh, even beautiful superior women think about crummy college boys who interrupt their lunch period to quote from biblical lessons that bored them in church. And anyway, I can see it in your eyes. You're wondering what sort of a world it is that gives me so much and you so little. But I'm wondering it, too. That's what I want to tell you."

"How do you know I'm not simply envying you? How do you know I'm not thinking that if I were in your shoes and came into such a windfall, I'd hire a manager for the iron works and take off for Paris and the life of Riley?"

I shook my head firmly. "Never. You'd stay here and improve the conditions of the workers."

Her eyes widened. "What makes you think I'm so philanthropic?"

"I saw that copy of the Debs news sheet you slipped into your handbag."

A pause followed this. "You're not going to tell Daddy, I trust."

"Of course I'm not going to tell Daddy. I hate Daddy."

"Nat Chisolm! What a thing to say!"

"Well, do you want the truth or don't you? What I'm trying to tell you is that I'm on *your* side."

She stared. "And what side is that?"

"Isn't that for you to say?"

I had made progress. Ellen began to take me seriously. We had earnest talks about working conditions in the mills, and she sought to educate me on the role I might one day play in providing shorter hours and higher pay and even in allowing a union which Father never had. She proved extremely knowledgeable in such matters, and I affected a greater interest than I felt. What did I have in mind? Did I want to marry Ellen? I don't believe I ever thought that far. I was, as I have said, dazzled by her, infatuated with her. I had never imagined having a close relationship with a woman of character and intellect so superior to my own. Did I want to sleep with her? Of course, but it did not seem like a feasible objective.

I was soon made aware of another obstacle. There was a man in Ellen's life. I had noticed that she wrote long letters at odd moments in the office, secreting each until finished under the blotter of her desk. One afternoon, when I had to go into town to deliver a document to the mayor's office, I was bold enough to pick up the stamped envelope lying on her desk and ask her if she wished me to mail it.

"That would be very kind," she replied, eyeing me sharply.

I had the impertinence to glance at the address. It was to a James Farmer in Pittsburgh.

"Who's this Jim? Somebody special?"

"Perhaps you'd like to read it."

I departed with a shrug, but the next day at our sandwich lunch I reverted to the subject.

"What does Mr. Farmer do? Of course I realize it's none of my business."

"Of course, it isn't. But I haven't the least objection to telling you. He's foreman in the rolling room of a steel mill."

"And does he share your concern for the common man?"

"You might even say he inspired it."

"Is that what you write him about?"

"No. I write him about an inquisitive young fellow called Nathaniel Chisolm."

"Doesn't that make him jealous?"

"Jim is above jealousy."

"Because he's too grand, too noble?"

"Because he's too big for petty emotions."

She was serious! My throat was suddenly dry with jealousy. "Are you going to marry him?"

For a moment she appeared to be debating how most stingingly to put me down. "I don't think Jim's the marrying kind" was all she finally said.

"Then what's there in it for you?"

"Is marriage the only possible relationship between a man and a woman?"

"For a woman like you, yes."

"And what is a woman like me?"

"A good woman. A great woman!" I jumped to my feet, reckless now. "Don't throw yourself away on a selfish bastard like that! Wait for a decent man. Wait for *me!*"

Shocked, she stared down at the blotter on her desk. "Oh, Nat, there could never be anything like that between you and me."

"Why the hell not? Do you think I'm a child?"

"Far from it. But even if there was no question of Jim — which is not the case — there'd still be the question of our ages and social positions. You have a fine career before you and the chance to do many good and useful things. You must finish your education and take your proper place in society."

"Oh, stop it, Ellen!" Angry now and disgusted, I was ready to fling everything away. "I never gave a damn about the iron works or the conditions here. I only wanted to impress you. And I've never had any real intention to live in

Troy or be the manager my old man wants me to be. And anyway, I couldn't be. There's no future here for anyone. You must know that."

"You mean because of the automobile? But horseshoes aren't the only thing you can make with iron. The works could be converted to other uses."

"Maybe, but not while my old man's in charge. He's blind as a bat and stubborn as a mule. There's no telling him anything. He's borrowed insanely to buy out my aunts; he's hocked up to his ears. He'll be bust in a year's time."

"How can you be so sure?"

"Do you want to look at the stock books? Here's the key." Father had given it to me that morning to retrieve a particular certificate from his private file. I tossed it on her desk. "Be my guest at the fall of the House of Chisolm!"

And I flung out of the room in disgust.

Two days later, on a Sunday morning, Ellen did an unexpected thing. She called at the mansion, but did not ask to see me, simply delivering a note suggesting that I join her that afternoon for a walk along the riverbank. I was to meet her, if I wished, at the main gate of the iron works, and needless to say, I was there at the appointed time.

It was a beautiful afternoon, warm and clear, and we strolled for two miles along the gently wooded bank of the river just south of the works. Our talk was desultory, and Ellen would occasionally stop to pluck a wild flower, and once we paused for several minutes to watch two herons fishing below us. It was evident that she had something serious to tell me, but I thought it better to let her bring it out at her own time and place. At last she turned to scramble up a fairly steep incline, and we found ourselves on a grassy ledge with a fine view over the water from which we were safe from any chance pedestrian eye. Here she spread her cape on the ground and sat down.

"You've been here before," I said as I squatted beside her. "Is this one of Jim's rendezvous?"

This seemed to give her her cue, for it all came out now in a rush.

"Look, Nat. You were dead right about the company. Things are in an even worse state than you thought. Your father's been applying desperately for bank loans." Her fingers pulled up a clump of crabgrass. "If the Bank of Commerce comes through, it may plug the leaks for a while. But it doesn't look to me as if the bank is coming through."

I had a strange feeling of elation. "And then what? Bankruptcy?"

"Unless someone takes over the works. There are a couple of offers, but they want your father's stock for almost nothing. Does he have any assets outside the company?"

"Not that I know of. I believe even the mansion is part of the works."

"Oh, Nat, what will he do?"

I extended my right forefinger and pointed it to my temple. "Click-click."

She gasped. "How can you be so horrible?"

"Well, hasn't the company been his whole life? What else does he have to live for? But no, Ellen, don't take me literally. I'm being dramatic, with my usual Trojan bad taste. Father'll survive. He's too tough to kill."

I was about to tell her of Grandpa Chase's fortune when I suddenly paused. Something flickered across the back of my mind to warn me that I was encountering a new feeling in Ellen, perhaps even the start of a sympathy for me.

"And what about *you?*" she inquired. "What's going to happen to you? Will you be able to go back to Harvard if everything goes to smash?"

"Who cares about Harvard? I'll get a job. There are other iron works, and better-run ones, presumably. I know the trade."

"But you *should* care about Harvard! You shouldn't have to be an operator. A career like yours mustn't be nipped in the bud. You should finish your education and go to work to help make factories less awful!"

"Well, it doesn't look as if things are coming out that way, does it? But what the hell, Ellen. Look at your own life. It hasn't exactly been a bed of roses, has it?"

"But I was born poor. I had to make my own way. Oh, I'm not saying you won't make yours. Of course you will. But all this is very hard on someone your age."

"It's not so hard with friends. Good friends." Here I took her hand. When she didn't resist, I leaned over boldly and kissed her on the lips. But I might have been kissing her cheek for all the response I got. She seemed lost in thought.

"Nat," she said at last, squeezing my hand hard and looking straight at the ground, "there's something I want to tell you. Something I thought about all last night after reading those files. I'll be leaving Troy now. I shan't wait for things to go to pot. It's very likely we won't meet again. But I want you to know that I believe in you. I think you may accomplish something one day. And I'd like to leave you with a pleasant memory of me. Let's not talk about love. Let's be simple. You've shown a man's interest in me, and I'm ready to respond with a woman's interest in you. Which is why I suggested this walk."

I turned very red and jumped to my feet. "You mean you want me to make love to you? Here and now?"

"Must we call it love? But yes, here and now. If you want to, of course."

"If I *want* to!"

"Then help me, please, with these buttons."

I'm afraid I tore some of them off. The world had turned
topsy-turvy, but that could be figured out later. Our encounter, for that seems the best word to describe it, was
unlike anything that ever happened to me, before or since.
Ellen, suddenly and unbelievably naked, proved pudgier
and perhaps older than I had imagined, but she had fine
alabaster skin and firm breasts with large nipples, and I took
quick advantage of my unexpected good fortune. Her re-
sponses, however, were disappointing; they seemed only
mechanical. At my first coming, too rapid, this hardly mat-
tered, but on the second time I found myself more aggressively trying to arouse some sensation in her, until in the
end our action was more like a rape than a union.

Afterwards, while she busied herself at the waterside with
some kind of prophylactic process, I turned sadly away to
the woods. It was as if I were seeking in nature the tender-
ness that had taken flight from the scene of our copulation.
The iron works seemed to have reached down the bank to
enfold us.

3

Ellen quit her job the next day, a Monday,
and left town without leaving a forwarding
address at her boardinghouse. On Tuesday
morning, when I came down to breakfast, I
found Father, who had already finished his, rather grimly
awaiting me.

"Perhaps you'd like some coffee, Nathaniel, before you
read a letter I want to show you."

I picked up the cup which our ever mournful butler had
placed before me. "A letter from whom?"

"From Miss Hardy, who recently demonstrated the civility of her class of women by quitting our employ without notice. It is addressed to one James Farmer in Pittsburgh, suspected of illegal unionizing in a steel plant there."

I glanced at the paper which the butler had now taken from Father and silently laid at my place. The handwriting was not Ellen's; it was presumably a copy. "Why is it proper for me to read a letter not addressed to me? Or to you, either, sir?"

"Because it behooves the owners and managers of businesses on which the general welfare depends to protect them from plotting anarchists. Our undercover man has had his eye on Miss Hardy for some weeks now. He opened this letter which she had placed in the mailbox in the reception hall, copied it and then sent it on."

I wanted to crumple it up and toss it back across the table to him, but curiosity mastered me. Now I read the following:

Jim, dearest, your suspicions were quite correct.
There's no point starting a union here. I had seen the signs of doom, but I wasn't sure till young Chisolm told me his aunts had pulled out and showed me the books to prove it. He's not a socialist, just a hot kid who wants to make me. Would that *you* did! More, I mean. And now, love, I'm coming back. But please, please, let me stay a while before the next job. I know you hate me to be "slobby," but it's been awfully lonely here.

I sat for some minutes in silence, indifferent to Father's baleful stare. So that was it. Ellen had used me from the beginning. She had not deemed me worthy to play a role in the radical mission of which her noble lover was an exalted leader. Oh, no! I was just a randy kid whose ruttishness could be used in espionage. And then tossed the cheap tip of a roll in the hay. Why not? What were sexual morals but bourgeois values? The enlightened woman was happy to spread her legs for any man who had helped the cause.

My love, if that was the word for it, was converted to a furious resentment. Ellen was promoted to the hate I felt for Father. The latter now spoke as I threw down the letter.

"Were you aware, when you took the astonishing liberty of informing Miss Hardy of our family security transactions, that she was a political radical?"

"I was."

"And was it your intention to warn me of her propensities?"

"Never."

"May I ask why?"

Everything in me had been seething and popping like molten iron. That Father, who had denigrated me all my life, should now be more right about Ellen than I had been was more than I could bear. I knew I was going to hurt him and hurt him hard, and it didn't matter to me if the blow should boomerang. My explosion had the relief of a suicide.

"Because I approved what she was doing! Because I wanted to help her! Because I wanted a union here to check your high and mighty way of running things!"

Father passed a quick hand over his eyes. "Go to your room, Nathaniel. Please. I'll need time to decide how I'm going to handle this."

"You won't have to handle it at all!" I leaped to my feet. "Because I'm leaving this house. Right this minute! And I'm never coming back! And I'm never going to take another penny from you as long as I live!"

Father gaped. "How *will* you live?"

"I don't know! And I don't care!"

.   .   .

I was good to my word about leaving, and the very next day I decamped for Albany where I shared a room with my old high school friend Alec Storrs, who was working in a department store there. He induced his employers to give me a job (probably by hinting that it might one day prove worth their while), and I was able to subsist without appealing to Mother, who was anyway out of ready communication, cruising on a diabeah with Grandfather and Bella up the Nile to see the temple at Abu Simbel. And even had she been available, I doubt that I should have called to her. What had happened was between Father and myself. She was irrelevant to it — I think I even felt that she might be somehow contaminated by it. She was, as I have said, the spirit of pleasure, and he of duty, and never the twain should meet. I have also said that she represented life and he its opposite. And now this contrast was to be even more grimly marked.

What my future would have been had these conditions continued I cannot imagine, but the passage of only a month brought about the event which decisively changed my life. Father shot himself through the temple in his office in the iron works one night when he was alone in the administration building. The banks had finally refused to bail him out, and he had understood that another week would bring his company to bankruptcy and receivership.

It may have been the memory of my grim jest to Ellen of the exact method of Father's death that got me through those first black days. It gave a kind of preordained reality to his tragedy that seemed to place it beyond my personal responsibility. For if the bankruptcy had been inevitable, given the company's financial impasse, and Father's decision not to survive it a necessary consequence, what effect on the succession of events could be attributed to his discovery of my treachery over the stock books and his shock at my apostasy and desertion? I could cling to the rag of my own non-involvement, and on that long night in Alec's room when he helped me to finish off a bottle of whiskey, he listened patiently while I ranted on about not even returning to Troy for the funeral.

"I don't ever want to see the damn place again!" I cried. "Why should I? It's never brought me anything but pain and misery. If Father chose to make a bloody mess of his business and a bloodier one of himself, that was his affair. I've got my own life to put together now. And I'm glad that I'll never owe him a damn penny! I wouldn't take one from his estate if it had one."

"You know you have to go home, Nat. If for no other reason than for your ma's sake. Drink all you want and rave all you want — that's fine — but in the end you know you'll have to go."

And of course I did. Unless I wanted to change my name and grow a beard and disappear into a drab eternity of roadside bars, there was no escaping a family rite of such gravity. I returned to Troy to find the mansion as efficiently and impersonally maintained as if Father were still in charge. Grandpa Chase, already headed west on the high seas with Mother, had cabled that he would be responsible for all household bills and that things should be in readiness for the widow and himself.

All I could do was roam about the big house and wait. The lawyers were in charge of all matters, but it was kindly suggested that I, an executor, might more usefully employ my time by going through Father's personal and family files. These were all as neat and orderly as might have been imagined, and I felt his bleak eye on me as I listlessly thumbed through them. Meticulous records had been kept of everything; I could have learned, had I wanted, just what the housekeeper had spent for butter ten years before and how many times the garden hoses had been mended. And all for what? A huge rummage sale!

But when putting the files back in the big cedar closet, I noticed one I had overlooked which bore the tab "Chisolm, Nathaniel Barton," and my heart tightened with foreboding. It appeared at first to contain only vital statistics — entries of childhood illnesses and inoculations, school grades and teachers' reports — but in the back was an envelope marked "Character and Fitness." It was the perusal of its contents that proved my undoing.

Father had made annual assessments of the development of my character. They were entered in his round, clear, curiously innocent handwriting, and must have been copied from drafts, for there was not a single erasure or interlineation. My good and bad traits were judicially balanced, but, to my surprise, the scales tipped in favor of the former. Father found me self-willed, stubborn, averse to authority, little prone to natural affections, lacking in all forms of courtesy and probably more than averagely subject to temptations of the flesh. He also found me honest, straightforward, courageous and (when my interest was aroused) capable of hard and efficient work. "Nathaniel may yet turn out to be a gentleman, in the best sense of that often ill-used term."

But what affected me most was a comment which he had added to the file just before I had started my summer job the previous June:

> I am beginning to hope that the confusion engendered in Nathaniel by his last trip to Paris and the contrast which Mr. Chase's Gallic atmosphere offers to the home sobriety may not be wholly deleterious. I suspect that he is beginning to see through his worldly grandsire and to be less dazzled by French nick-nacks and immoralities. I can only

regret that Eliza's excesses of demonstrated affection and
her insistence on spoiling her children have required me to
hold my own feelings for Nathaniel in such constant
check. I look forward to the day when he shall have graduated from the necessary rigors of a masculine education,
and my dear son and I may clasp hands as partners in life.

My first reaction was an exploding anger at the idiocy of a
system of educating a boy imposed on Father by some fool
puritan tradition or dusky god — or simply by his own
warped nature. How could he have had the folly to encase
himself in that black suit of armor and slam the visor shut
over eyes and lips that might have smiled at me? Love?
Could you really call it love if it had no tongue, no gleam of
an eye, no outstretched hand? Did a poem exist if it was
never put on paper? Or an idea, if it was not communicated?

And then a black little thought began to trickle forward
from the recesses of my fevered mind. Had Father *not*
reached out to me? Had I not, again and again, spurned that
timidly offered hand, made him feel a fool for his pains? I
began to recall hesitant gruff bids that he and I should do
this or that together, small things like walking to the works
in the morning or joining him for a cigar on the verandah
after dinner, and my invariably conjuring up some insult-
ingly inadequate excuse. I had assumed that he didn't really
want my company, but now I could see it might have been
more the case that I had been watching for chances to snub
him and had found enough of them to discourage him at last
from further tentatives. After all, he was proud. Almost as
proud as I was.

Now the picture that I had been desperately warding off
flooded my mind with hideous illumination. I saw Father
sitting alone at midnight at his desk in the deserted office
building, poring over the ledgers that announced his doom
and reaching at last into the drawer for the fatal weapon.

O God! When a word from me would have saved him. If I could only have been there to cry: "Father, you and I can build another business! See if we don't!"

For two days I didn't speak to a soul. I ate my brief meals in silence and trudged for miles along the riverbank. When I passed the scene of my "encounter" with Ellen, I reflected that even in that cool relationship I had been the cooler partner. For had I not taken advantage of her pity by allowing her to think that the failure of the iron works would make me a pauper? And had she not been simply generous in lending her body to the consolation of a young man about to lose his education and his future? Ellen had had a heart. Where had mine been?

There is no telling what sort of state I might have worked myself into had Mother not suddenly arrived, having been driven up to Troy at night, with Grandpa and Bella, directly from the pier in New York where their ship had docked. She burst into the house, a lovely flurry of blue silk (she would wear mourning only at the memorial service), and hugged me tightly and long before she uttered a word. It was like the opening of the doors in the first act of *Die Walküre* when the glory of the moonlit forest fills the scene.

"My darling, darling boy, who has borne all this horror alone! I'll never leave you again! Never, never!"

Mother had always a strong layer of common sense beneath the sparkle and froth of her exterior; she knew where her priorities lay. She had been exceedingly fond of her difficult husband — the physical attraction between them had never quite died — but she saw his suicide as a repudiation not only of life but of everything in life that was to her worthwhile, including herself. There was nothing she could do about the dead; her job was with the living. She set about at once to pull me out of the rapids of despond which were loosening my grip on rationality.

"I didn't even hear of your leaving home and going to Albany until we got back from Egypt. Oh, Nat, you must go up the Nile one day. It's so glorious! But of that later. Your grandfather took some wonderful photographs. When I got your father's letter at last about your running off — he didn't bother to cable — my first thought was: what about Harvard? Will he miss a term? Of course you must go right back. Grandpa has a friend who's very close to President Lowell — he can explain everything. Anyway, my first thought when I got your father's letter was that I must go straight to you, and I was actually on the telephone engaging a stateroom when Grandpa came in with the terrible news of what had happened."

The lawyers, the household, the very order of the memorial service, she turned over to Grandpa while she devoted herself entirely to me. Bella, who was now sixteen, had been sufficiently comforted and consoled on the steamer. Mother and I walked and sat on the porch and talked together for hours on end. When I showed her Father's notes on my character, she seemed almost to lose her temper.

"Imagine his leaving those papers behind for you to read! Was he *trying* to ruin your life with remorse? If he loved and admired you — and I have no doubt he did, in his own peculiar way — he should have told you so in his lifetime. But to leave a booby trap like that! No, no, my love, it won't do! Oh, I see I shall have to go right on fighting him. He's spoiled enough of your life with his foolish theories of manliness. And he isn't going to spoil another day of it while I have a breath in my body!"

In the battle for my conscience she enlisted my grandfather's aid, and I must admit the old boy was very convincing.

"You say your father meant well, Nat. But I could never excuse a man who hurt me by meaning well. Had I been a heretic in Toledo, should I have excused the grand inquisitor for burning me at the stake because he thought it was God's will? Never! In judging any act, we must take into account the result of it, good or bad, as well as the intent, good or bad. If I seek to ruin you with a false market tip, and it turns out to make you a fortune instead, is that a good act on my part? Hardly. Well, then, if a good result won't excuse a bad intent, why should a good intent excuse a bad result? Your father had no business allowing his mind to be cluttered with inane theories of how to bring up a son. *That* I can never excuse."

That night, lying awake into the small hours, I came to a resolution to which I believe I have been largely faithful ever since. I vowed that I was not going to allow my poor misguided father to have died in vain. I resolved to profit by his example. I would stoutly resist all temptations to make hash of my health and happiness. I would ruthlessly exterminate any last traces of the puritan in my blood. I would seize from life all that it had to offer me of material and immaterial prizes. I would have beauty in my existence: in whatever profession I should practice, in the woman I should love, in the family I should raise, in the art and books in which I should steep myself, and maybe in the very god whom I should worship, even if I had to create him myself!

4 Deciding, no doubt correctly, that the island of Manhattan was where she truly belonged, Mother leased a Beaux Arts mansion on East Seventieth Street and entered Bella in Miss Chapin's School. The house suffered from the pompousness of the nineties and was really adapted only for entertainment. But this was just what Mother wanted. She loved its ballroom and "state" dining room, though they took up so much space and were so bleak when not in use that Bella and I felt somehow huddled on the outskirts of prospective or retrospective galas. Without Mother it would have been depressing, but she made every corner where she happened to be almost cozy. She could have made us enjoy a picnic on the marble stairs.

I had returned to Harvard, of course, but with a new wardrobe and a new outlook on life. I had even become something of a dandy. It was too late for me to be admitted to a "good" club, and I had certainly no intention of dropping the unfashionable friends of my previous incarnation (though they tended to drift away from the now sartorial Nat), but I managed to establish myself as one of the leaders of what I liked to consider a free-thinking, innovative group, made up of refugees from both the stiff social undergraduate right wing and the too sober and humorless left. We thought of ourselves as witty and uncommitted hedonists, flaunting a daring aestheticism. We must have been very silly indeed.

Mother, anyway, didn't see us that way. She found my new friends delightful and invited them to stay with her whenever they came to New York, whose parties and theaters were much more to their liking than anything Cambridge offered. It may seem odd that we were so intent on amusing ourselves when the Great War was now raging in Europe, but opinion on our side of the Atlantic had not yet hardened against the Central Powers, and there was considerable feeling, at least in my set, that we should not be drawn in. It was my one bone of contention with Mother, whose long visits abroad had made her passionately pro-French.

"You want to feed me and my friends into those horrible trenches," I mocked her. "You want us to die for your rides in the Bois and your tea and *petits fours* with duchesses in the old Faubourg."

"Oh, darling boy, don't even joke about such things!" She gave a little shriek of dismay. "But you can't want to see those ghastly Krauts goose-stepping down the Champs-Elysées, can you?"

"Isn't their desire to do that a kind of compliment to Paris? Aren't they basically envious of French culture? And isn't it just what they need? Mightn't a united France and Germany be a greater nation than either?"

"Horrors! I should never have taken you to Germany. That's something of your father in you, I'm afraid. He actually liked those people. Well, God preserve the French from German envy, if that's what it is. Can't you just see the *sales Boches* stamping their boots over the City of Light and then wanting to know who put the light out? But, my angel boy, I was never talking about sending *you* or any of your friends overseas. It's only *economic* help the Allies need. Talk to Percy Maxwell. He'll tell you all about it."

But I *had* talked to the Honorable Percival Maxwell about it. He was the British consul general in New York and an old friend of Mother's from her Paris days when he had been chargé there. And I had to admit he was the highest type of English aristocrat, finely intelligent and startlingly broad-minded, lean and bony with brown crinkled skin and small twinkling azure eyes, who had been everywhere, read everything and knew everyone. A widower of fifty, he had two sons in the war to whose trials (or to his own) he never made reference.

I had seen too many men hovering about Mother not to have learned to mask a filial resentment at flirtations that even Hamlet would have perceived as innocent. Mother, a basic puritan, suffered from simple greediness: she wanted to have her cake of frilly romantic dabbling and eat it too, in the sense of having her admirers not ask for more. With her charm she usually managed to pull this off, though I can recall a couple of surly, perhaps justifiably indignant gentlemen stalking out of the Paris house. The Honorable Percival, however, was perfect; he gave every appearance of being serenely content with the *amitié amoureuse* that was all she appeared to offer him.

But I had a different bone to pick with Mr. Maxwell. It was perfectly evident that his principal job for king and country was to embroil us in the war, and no amount of reassuring chatter about Britain's seeking only our money and guns could conceal her desperate need for total American participation. My trouble was that I could not see the war as one for civilization. As Mother had implied, I had found as a boy the atmosphere of Germany friendly, healthy, even exhilarating, as opposed to the chilly aloofness of England and the indifference and graspingness of the French. Nor could I understand, though people around me were beginning to raise their hands and voices in protest, why a blockaded Germany was not justified in sinking without warning *any* belligerent merchant vessel, or why, if Americans had chosen to sail on the *Lusitania*, they had not done so at their own risk. Indeed, I went so far as to suspect that the horrors of trench warfare were Britain's price for hanging on to a bloated empire whose riches were little shared by her embattled Tommies.

I didn't say any of this, of course, to Mr. Maxwell. I didn't have to. He easily divined my attitude and was far too clever to dispute it directly. In fact, in his easy relations with me he seemed to make a point of avoiding any discussion of the war, preferring instead to talk of French literature, which I had elected as my major subject at Harvard. He seemed particularly interested in what I had to say about Marcel Proust, whose first novel, *Du Côté de chez Swann*, had appeared in 1913.

"One of the wretched things about this war is that I have so little time to read," Maxwell said. "Is it really a new chapter, as some claim, in the history of the novel?"

"Well, I doubt there's ever been another writer who could evoke the past as vividly as he does."

"Ah, the past." Maxwell sighed. "But isn't it a book about jealousy?"

"In part. Proust thinks jealousy and love are the same thing. Of course that's twaddle, but he almost convinces you. Almost, but not quite. To me, love must be pleasure. Or it's not love."

"Ah, yes, you're a great hedonist, I know." Maxwell nodded. "There's not much room for that in poor old Europe these days. No doubt it will come back in time."

My isolationist principles were not inconsistent with a decent human sympathy. "It must seem very trivial to you, sir, my reading Proust while your sons are fighting."

"Not at all, dear boy. Not at all. We must keep the lamp of culture alight. Or else, what's it all about?"

One night in the spring vacation, when I was leaving one of Mother's parties after dinner to go on to a gathering in the

Village, I encountered Mr. Maxwell in the hall, also departing early, being helped into his evening cloak by our butler. Taking the cane that was now handed to him, he turned to me.

"It's a fine evening, Nathaniel. Would you care to stroll down the avenue? We might even stop for a libation at the Knickerbocker Club."

I was about to plead my engagement when I noted the haggard look of the drawn skin under his eyes. I found myself nodding and taking his elbow as we went down the front steps together.

I had expected that we might exchange polite nothings about the party, but we didn't. We walked in silence down the park side of Fifth Avenue the half-dozen blocks to his club.

"Would you come in for a drink?" When I was again about to demur, he added: "I'd take it kindly."

In a corner of the big red leathery empty barroom we sat silently before our whiskies. At last he spoke.

"I received a cable just before going to your mother's. My son Eric was killed in the Somme. You may ask why I went to the dinner. Because of her guest of honor, Señor Endara. Argentina is an important and at times a doubtful neutral."

"But how appalling for you," I murmured.

"It's not easy. Some have had it worse. And my other boy, Alistair, is out of it now, though minus the leg he lost at Ypres. The job here, fortunately, keeps me distracted."

"Did Eric have a family?"

"No, thank heavens. I had just the two of them. Alistair, anyway, has a wonderful girlfriend. And something may come of it if he'll only get over his silly notion that a one-legged chap has no business asking a woman to share his life."

I shook my head in a sudden fit of self-disgust. "What must you think of my generation living it up over here while all that goes on!"

"Do you know something, Nat? It may all be for the best. Oh, of course, I'm not supposed to say that, and I won't again after tonight. We need you all in this mess, and we need you badly. But just for this one hour, and because I'm so devoted to your mother, let me say that it might be a better thing for civilization if one generation of fine young men like yourself were to survive this war and help restore the poor old battered globe."

"If there's anything left to restore."

"Aye, there's the rub." Mr. Maxwell pinched his eyelids slowly with two fingers of his left hand. "We may be paying too high a price for victory." He coughed and straightened himself up in his chair. "There. I've said it, and I've said enough. I trust you won't quote me."

"You shall not trust in vain."

"One can't help one's doubts, but one *can* help expressing them. Still, the circumstances may excuse this one little outbreak. Good! I feel better already. And now, young man, you've done your day's good deed. Be off to your revels!"

But the idea of going on to a silly party and leaving him alone to mourn his gallant son was abominable to me. With the quick reversals of youth, my heart now pounded with sympathy for this tragic but unbroken man. I suddenly wanted to give him everything I had. I actually offered him Mother!

"If you should ever become my stepfather, I'd try to be another Eric to you."

I suppose it was the only thing in the world I could have said that at that moment should have made him laugh in sheer surprise.

"Oh, my dear fellow, you don't have to go *that* far. Now this is really enough. I'm going to get a cab and go straight home."

The result of this incident was that I quit college for the second time to volunteer as a driver for the Harvard Unit of the U.S. Ambulance Corps in France. An action so diametrically opposed to my newfound philosophy of discriminating pleasure-seeking I can only attribute to the explosion of the natural emotions that I had supposed were under lock and key in the comely mansion of my aestheticism. The desire to identify myself with all the gore and suffering that threw my undergraduate life into such horrid relief was as overwhelming as it was unreasonable. I had not changed my mind about the war; I had simply become ashamed of my immunity. It was too strong a thing to combat; indeed, it seemed almost something to wallow in. Perhaps that would be the last, the ultimate pleasure: to lose oneself in Armageddon because Armageddon made any other course seem so contemptible.

Mother was distraught. She came up immediately to Boston where we met in her suite in the Ritz.

"But why, my child, why in the name of God can't you at least wait until we get into the war? Percy himself says it's only a matter of months."

"How can he tell? Didn't Wilson win on the plank that he kept us out of it? And anyway, if we do get in, they tell me I can transfer to the army. So why wait?"

"Why?" she wailed. "To save your precious life for a few months, that's why. And you don't even believe in what they're fighting for!"

"Oh, but I do. I've been converted." I laughed at her look of dismay. "And it was you who did it. You taught me the charm of decadent empires. Those long lazy Edwardian afternoons on greenswards by rose-pink Jacobean mansions. Those gracefully moldering châteaux surrounded by lily-padded moats —"

"Oh, hush, hush!" She jumped up to put a hand to my mouth. "How can you make mock of everything at a time like this? If I thought Percy was responsible for what you're doing —"

"Well, he's not," I interrupted firmly. "He thinks I should stay home and preserve the arts of peace."

Poor Mother! There was little she could do. The only thing she asked of me that I couldn't refuse was to sit for a charcoal sketch by a famous Boston artist. It turned out to be a very handsome picture indeed — far more so than its model — and was later used on an enlistment poster. I think that had I died in France, Mother would have derived a not inconsiderable consolation in gazing at it and showing it proudly to all and sundry. She loved me, I knew, but she always had in her the stuff of survivors. And beautiful things played a role in her life not too far behind beautiful people.

A minimum of training was required for ambulance drivers, but red tape also had its function, and it was some months before I found myself crossing the ocean on a merchant vessel constantly alerted by U-boat alarms. The passage, however, was without actual incident except the news on our radio that President Wilson had called for a declaration of war. When we docked in Le Havre I felt rather a fool.

I had a few free days before reporting to the transport office which would send me to a base hospital near the front at Verdun, and I spent one of them with Grandpa Chase in Paris. He had elected to remain abroad during the war, and I had expected to find him as shrilly belligerent as most expatriates in the capital were. I had been told that the war spirit was as high in the spacious mansions of the elderly American noncombatants as it was low among the poor poilus in the trenches, and I had fully expected to be slapped on the back and dispatched enthusiastically to the zone of peril by a sparkling old gentleman insisting that he envied me. Nothing could have been further from the case. I found Grandpa lonely and depressed. He saw that I was served an excellent dinner, but he partook of little of it, contenting himself with glass after glass of champagne.

"I would have stopped you from coming over, dear boy, if I'd been warned in time." He had waited until his butler was out of the room, but even so he dropped his voice to a hoarse whisper. He shook his head sadly and ruffled his long white hair with a nervous hand. "Or at least done everything in my power to stop you. Things are frightful where you're headed. The French are having to shoot deserters by the dozen."

"Surely our coming in will buoy them up, won't it?" I exclaimed.

"If it's not too late. But hmm." He gave me a warning wink as the butler reappeared. "We're all very proud of this young man, aren't we, Pierre?"

"*Très fier, monsieur. Et avec les Américains la victoire est assurée.*"

The old boy raised his glass in a toast to victory, and after a sip I handed mine to Pierre so he could join in it. But afterwards, alone with me in the great dark library, Grandpa waxed gloomily confidential again.

"I very much fear you're walking into a stalemate, Nat. There are no victories in trench warfare. Haig and Foch don't hesitate to sacrifice a hundred thousand men to gain a few yards of mud or to straighten out a dent in a salient. It's a kind of lunatic game of chess where winning has no relation to the cost in lives. In every offensive the attackers lose twice what the defenders do. Yet the high brass doesn't have the sense to sit tight."

"Sit tight until what happens, sir?"

"Until one side or the other cracks. Or until the war-obsessed governments agree to a compromise."

"But if the Germans win, won't we have surrendered the world to militarism?"

"Militarism! What are Haig and Foch but militarism? What is militarism but shooting men who prefer not to die for a patch of land — how does Hamlet put it — 'which is not tomb enough and continent to hide the slain'?"

"But even if what you say is true, there isn't much I can do about it now, is there?"

"Of course there is. I wouldn't have brought it up other-wise. We're in this war now. Every able-bodied young American is needed for military service. Leave the ambu-lance driving to old Frenchmen. Tell your field unit you want to ship home for officers' training. That you'd never have signed up for this if you'd known your country was going to war. They'll be glad enough to let you go. And if not, I'll talk to our ambassador. I'll tell him I want my only grandson to be a hero, not a chauffeur! People may even admire you. And you will have gained six months, maybe a year. Who knows? The damn fool war may be over by then."

"But my unit's going to the front, Grandpa! The guys would think I'm running away. And wouldn't I be?"

But there was certainly sense in what Grandpa counseled. He was offering me the opportunity to correct the first seri-ous mistake I had made in my life, a mistake into which I had been induced by sheer sentimentality, the sprite whose dangerous allure I had soberly assessed in the dark days in Troy after Father's suicide. My new philosophy had not required me to avoid the civic obligations of my generation, but to avoid the folly of anticipating them. How ridiculous to have come rushing over to Europe to perform a perilous task that any middle-aged Frenchman could do as well, when to have awaited my country's call to arms would have perfectly satisfied every standard of patriotism and spared me months of exposure to German shells. Truly, I had been an ass and richly deserved to be blown to bits on my first day at the front.

But there it was. I couldn't go back. I think I can honestly say that it was not fear of my unit's reproach, spoken or unspoken. I certainly would not have reproached one of them, should he have adopted such a course. It was simply that the picture of Nat Chisolm turning away from danger after offering to confront it was repulsive to me. I would have preferred death.

And Grandpa, too, understood this after we had discussed it more fully.

"It's perfectly true that we can never be wholly rational," he conceded at last. "I once turned down a promising client — the heir to a great fortune and title — because I happened to know that in the days before some fortuitous family deaths had improved his prospects, he had cheated at cards."

The countryside where the second battle of Verdun was fought hardly answered to that term. "No man's land" was the more apt description of the front; it resembled the crater of a volcanic explosion, the bleak desert of a diseased imagination. Houses that were still recognizable as such were mere roofless walls and gaping windows. Not so much as a green thing or a tree trunk was left standing. The whole brown valley with its dirt roads was a mess of shell holes; a man could not walk six feet in a row without stumbling into one. Those on the roads were constantly being refilled, but driving an ambulance with its cargo of wounded was difficult, at times impossible. The small hills on either side of the valley were covered with guns, and the flashing, streaking sky at night was like some Fourth of July of demon gods.

One night, six weeks after my arrival in this hell hole, driving a car with two near corpses back to the base camp, I heard the whine of a shell too close and leaped from the vehicle to roll into the nearest hole. My ambulance was disintegrated. I could only huddle in my shelter and wait for dawn. Though the battle raged all over the valley, I was strangely and eerily alone.

That was the first and only time in my life that I knew absolute terror. Had I been required in that next hour to move, stand up, obey a command of any sort, I should have been physically incapable. I was paralyzed except for my quaking. It was as if I were the lone survivor of that terrible battle and was awaiting the shell that would surely find me at last and whose arrival I both hideously dreaded and desperately craved. That death would mean the annihilation of both spirit and body I doubted not any more than I do today. And had I been offered my deliverance from that field of horror at the cost of victory for the Kaiser and German occupation of the Allied nations, I would have nodded my head eagerly to the chorus of my chattering teeth.

Fortunately for our side, no such bargain was offered by the gods of war, and by dawn I was able to get hold of myself and totter back to our base camp. There I found there was no ambulance available for me, and I was sent down from the front with the remnants of my unit. I was informed that I could now apply for repatriation if I wished to be a candidate for officers' training school, and I did so. As it turned out, I was in Fort Devens in Massachusetts when the armistice was declared. Grandpa's prediction had come true, after all.

I did not go to any victory parties. I was convinced that the peace would be a vindictive one. I cared only to leave the war well behind me. Years later Noël Coward wrote in *Cavalcade* of the spirit of sacrifice in wartime which "made strange heaven out of unbelievable hell." I had not found the strange heaven, nor was I going to waste any time looking for it. I had deemed the war aims of both sides equally imperialistic and the whole conflict a conspiracy to eliminate joy from the planet. Lloyd George and Clemenceau were to me as blind as Father fighting to preserve the horseshoe in the age of the automobile. I thought I had learned my lesson about life at last.

Like Walter Pater's Marius I turned back to an enlightened epicureanism. I reconfirmed the resolution I had taken after Father's death. Only now I hoped to avoid any aspect of undergraduate impudence or show-off. I would rededicate my life to the highest and noblest pleasures. I would give due obeisance to the rules of good conduct needed for an orderly existence in crowded communities. I would show proper consideration to my fellow men and affection to my family and friends. I would perform my share of civic duties. But no more than my share. Not a jot. My first obligation would be to make a happy man of Nathaniel Chisolm. A very happy man. That was the only garden that I could hope to cultivate with any real chance of success.

5

As I look back on the north shore of Long Island in the early nineteen twenties — the opulent part I mean, that long string of many-acred estates that ran down the Sound in a seemingly unbroken row from Roslyn to Huntington, with its stately mansions of Georgian red brick or Palladian style — I may be seeing it through a haze of nostalgia. Yet it seems to me that it possessed a dignity and charm that approached the aristocratic. Newport was pompous and showy, even in spots downright vulgar; Southampton florid and tacky; Bar Harbor was dwarfed ridiculously by its sea and hills; and Greenwich reeked of the marketplace. But the north shore had the serene pride of the grandest bankers, of the House of Morgan; it scorned the gossipy chatter of the spa, the noisy matutinal reunions of the beach club. Its denizens met to hunt the fox or watch the polo or play croquet on wide level swards, withdrawing for tea or drinks on cool verandahs. It was before the day of overnight fortunes from pet foods or chain stores; the trustees of the Piping Rock and Creek clubs were the financial statesmen in whose hands the nation's welfare seemed secure. Nor did their wives appear in the Sunday rotogravure or in the columns of society reporters.

Or so it seemed to me. There was that side of it, anyway, or the appearance of such a side. Mother had married Percy Maxwell after the armistice and given up her city house for a noble colonial manor in Locust Valley designed for her by Delano & Aldrich; she and her new mate were already stalwarts of the society I have described. Bella and I occupied a wing of their new dwelling, and I was ready now to put in practice my new principles. I did not delay.

For two whole years I led the life of the exquisite bachelor. I fox-hunted in the fall, went south in the winter and played polo in the summer. Grandpa Chase had died and left me and Bella each a legacy that threw off an annual income of twenty-five thousand dollars. Mother, of course, got the residue. Luck seemed determined to smile at the three of us.

Percy, who had become my close friend as well as my stepfather, took it upon himself eventually to inquire about my future.

"Why must I have one?" I riposted.

"You would make a whole life out of pleasure?"

"Do you know of a higher goal? Or one more difficult to attain?"

He nodded doubtfully. "For a whole life? Difficult indeed."

"You think I should go to Wall Street?"

"Is that all a young man can do?"

"Make money, I mean. Why, if I have it already?"

"Enough? For a bachelor, I suppose. But yours is hardly a fortune, my dear boy, and when you marry and little Chisolms begin to appear on the scene —"

I interrupted. "Well, Mother's not exactly a pauper."

"Very true. But she has a feminine way of spending all her income. And it's not excessive, I need hardly tell you, in *her* set. I could be cozy in one room in a club, but your mama . . ." He shrugged expressively.

Of course he was right. Mother would never let me want for anything, but, like many heiresses of her generation, she hung back from sizable settlements on male offspring. She and her *consoeurs* had seen too many fortunes dissipated by the sons of business captains, either in Monte Carlo or on chorus girls, or, more decorously but just as fatally, in financial *culs-de-sac*, like Father's. Their economic trust was limited to the self-made.

"Still, I have what I need for now."

"And let us suppose for the moment it is enough for the future. It's still a question if an American can be happy in a life devoted to even a discriminating pursuit of delights. If you'd been born a French or Italian aristocrat, or even an English one of my generation, it might have been feasible. But the American full-time sportsmen, even the best of them like Harry Whitney, have a tendency to drink. They can never seem to divorce themselves from the Yankee work ethic."

"You challenge me to break new ground."

It was like Percy not to persist. He knew he could always come back to the subject at a better time. He had not been a diplomat for nothing.

What did, however, change my life was the advent of Alice Agnew. I had known her before I went to France and had enjoyed her pouty prettiness and saucy wit, but when I met her again on Long Island, she had developed into a beauty with all the easy assurance of one who sees it as a gift that is her due. She was like a Gibson girl with a touch of the flapper. She was tall and graceful of movement, with a fine pale oval countenance, a small nose with a tiny hook and brilliant mocking grey eyes. Even the fashionable bob in which she wore her golden hair seemed distinguished. She made no effort to conceal the fact that she found me a welcome addition to the youthful crowd that she easily dominated.

Her parents were elderly, in their early sixties, and regular members of that north shore society, even prominent in it, though not rich. They were a big, bony, stylish couple, too sure of themselves and their welcome everywhere, who lived in a tumbledown farmhouse in Old Westbury with a few fine relics of better days. Mr. Agnew, an overly persistent optimist, had lost a considerable inheritance as a stockbroker. Like my father, he had learned too late that he couldn't afford to work, and, reduced at last to the income of a small but unbreakable trust fund, he managed to eke it out at the bridge table despite a reputation of quitting when he was ahead and not always paying his losses. People put up with him because they liked "poor Doris," who was so brave about everything, and because . . . well, because they always had.

It was at one of Mother's Sunday lunches, attended by the Agnews and their only child, that Alice and I had our first serious talk. Seated beside me, she had suggested that I take her sailing that afternoon, and when I protested a polo engagement, which had been a previous excuse, she asked: "Can you play polo all your life?"

"I hope I can play it for a long time. Though I shouldn't care to, except at my peak."

"Even if it were almost your peak?"

"Even so."

"But surely a decline can be very slow. Perhaps barely perceptible. Indeed, how can you be sure it hasn't already started?" Her smile was not intended to soften the sting.

I shrugged. "I may have missed my calling. A bullfighter has a good chance of being killed before he declines."

"Why not choose chess and get better and better up to the bitter end?" She didn't wait for an answer. "But tell me, *is* there a life after polo?"

"It's still a wide world, even if it's shrinking. There's big-game hunting. And polar exploration. And then there's always Paris, isn't there?"

"*Is* there? You mean the arts? Do you write, paint? Are you what they call a renaissance man?"

"I've written some short stories. Perhaps one or two half-decent ones. And I've always sketched. I've even made some music."

"I see." Now she was pensive. "In other words, you'll do anything in the world but sell bonds."

"We're only sure of one life."

She glanced bleakly down the table to where her father was talking to his hostess. "*He's* never done anything with his. And he doesn't seem to regret it. Does that mean his finest impulses are totally dead? If he ever had any." She looked to see if I was interested and then continued. "Father says that young people always talk about having freer and bolder lives than their parents. That it's the sacred convention of youth. But he thinks only one in a thousand does. The others content themselves with some minor generational change, usually in sexual mores, and then crow that they're liberated."

"You think I claim to be that thousandth? I don't. I simply want to be in charge of my own act."

"But that's just it! That's the *rara avis.*" She looked at me more carefully now. "I wonder if you might really be it. Father doesn't think so."

"I didn't know he did me the honor to think of me at all."

"Oh, he knew your father. I think he even invested in his company. It would have been just his luck."

"He thinks I'll end up selling horseshoes? Or failing to sell them?"

"Wasn't it bonds we were talking about? He exempts you from the horseshoes."

"*Merci du compliment.*"

"He didn't mean it as such. I think he rather admired your father's failure. He said at least it was different."

"At least it wasn't a life at the card table."

But she was above vulgar loyalties. "Oh, Father's only boast is that he never really tried. He isn't even a failure."

Mother rose now, as the meal was over, and we all stood.

"I have no truck with Father's prognostications" was Alice's last comment as we walked out.

After this we started to go about together. I called her every morning on the assumption, which she seemed to accept, that we would plan a shared day. We might play golf or arrange tennis doubles or simply go to the beach club. If I was playing polo, she would come and watch. She was a good athlete and looked well at whatever she was doing; even on the tennis court on a humid day she hardly seemed to perspire. My preferred picture of those days is of her at the club swimming pool, her fine figure revealed in a skin-tight black silk bathing suit, tucking a last strand of hair under a white bathing cap before bounding down the board to leap into the air and execute a graceful swan dive.

Her conversation was terse and to the point.

"I'm not sure your mother really likes me," she told me once.

"What makes you think that?"

"She's too nice to me."

"Oh, but that's her way. She's perfectly sincere."

She might have found this a curious trait in an older woman, but she didn't reject it. "Mine so rarely is. Which may have warped my judgment. But she's perfectly sincere in believing that yours must mind our being such paupers."

"Mother doesn't think that much about money."

"Ah, that's being really rich. If you *knew* our shabby subterfuges. Or does everyone? I sometimes think they must."

"All I know is that you're the handsomest and best-turned-out girl on the north shore."

"But you don't know all the cadging, the borrowing, the unpaid bills!"

"I don't care, if you don't."

"But I do!" Her changes of subject were swift. "I'm glad anyway your mama is sincere. I do cotton to her. She showed me her love diary. The one she kept when Mr. Maxwell was courting her. Do you know, it's passionate!"

"Is that so surprising?"

"Then theirs is not a *mariage blanc?* I always suppose it must be when people that age marry."

"Mother lived a number of years in Paris. They take those things more seriously over there."

"Really?" Her laugh was drawling, even insolent. "And you don't mind the idea of your ma in the arms of the old Brit? I thought all sons did."

"Not a bit. I used to object to some of her callers in Paris. But now that she's married, it's different. You see, I'm a basic conservative."

"Is that a hint that I'll have to wait?"

"Oh, in your case I'll make an exception."

But she would not become one. Alice was a teaser; she was not willing to yield me more than a kiss, and rather a chaste one at that, before becoming officially engaged. Her candor might have been a game; I couldn't tell. And after a time I was too infatuated to care.

"I've been well brought up, you see," she announced tartly one evening when a sharp slap had been needed to keep me off. But her anger, if anger it was, died with the reproof. "Nobody is so well brought up as a poor girl in a rich society. Mummie keeps drumming it into my head that I've got only one thing to sell and that if I give it away, I'll end up in the streets. So thank you very much, I'd rather be Mrs. Nathaniel Chisolm than a prostitute."

"But are you really willing to be Mrs. Nathaniel Chisolm?"

"Is this the long-awaited proposal?"

I paused. "Not yet, I guess."

"That's right. Don't be rash. And anyway, I doubt Pa has got through checking your bank account. He says people are usually either a good deal richer or a good deal poorer than they appear, and with the Maxwells he suspects it may be the latter. He seems to think I might do better."

Alice and I were much admired as a couple. We were considered highly romantic, prototypes of the postwar era of liberated thinking and stylish attitudinizing. Was I in love with Alice at this time? Or she with me? Perhaps as much as either of us was ever to be. Neither of us, I am sure, had an eye for anyone else. If we were a bit self-consciously what people thought us, was that not part of any romance? How many lovers really get outside of themselves? We might have been egoists, but can't egoists fall in love?

When I told Mother that I was going to propose to Alice, her initial reaction was disappointing.

"Well naturally I love her — who doesn't? — but aren't you both a bit young? I don't so much mean in actual years as in experience. I mean you don't have a job, or really any very definite idea of what you want to do with your life. Dear boy, you're both still children!"

"How many children have been at Verdun?"

"But that wasn't life! That must have been a nightmare. Life is full of small dull things."

"Has *yours* been?"

"Oh, darling, if you only knew! I went through all kinds of trouble with your father and even with your poor old grandfather. My life may *look* easy, but it's taken a lot of well-concealed effort to give it that appearance."

"Look, Mother. I know the sort of female skills you're referring to. But do you think you have a monopoly on them? Don't you think Alice may have some too? She's not unlike you, you know."

Mother seemed struck by this. "It's certainly true that her family has managed extremely well." She thought for a minute. "And I daresay they've taught her what they know." She suddenly smiled. "And anyway, you're going to do what you want to do. Percy's all for it, and Percy's always right."

Alice and I became engaged to a resounding chorus of approval. She persisted in her act of Millamant in *The Way of the World*, affecting to take me against her better judgment, carried away by a feeling that had to be somewhat absurd. She might have said, like Congreve's lovely heroine: "Well, you ridiculous thing you, I'll have you." But it was generally believed that she was very much in love, and I think she was pleased to have conveyed that impression. Only my sister appeared to oppose the match, and her objections were voiced only to me.

Bella had had a miserable coming-out year. She was not bad looking, though too tall and too skinny; she had fine dark hair and large appealing dark eyes that wavered between sympathy and distrust. But she handled herself awkwardly and tended to talk either too much or too little. She was easily put off, easily hurt, and she had a tendency to bolt upstairs and slam her bedroom door. In our world few of the young men could be bothered to make much effort with diffident girls, and those who did were apt to be from the impecunious fringe and suspected of mercenary motives. Bella's basic problem was Mother. Had Mother been less beguiling, Bella might have rebelled, gone to college, made some serious radical friends and found herself. But Mother's constant appeals to her — "Darling, it won't be any fun for *me* if you don't come along" or "Now *this* time I'll promise to go to all the places *you* want" — enmeshed the poor girl in the maternal gaieties and excursions until she began to fear she would end an old maid who had never lived, the kind who submit at last to become a mumbling chorus of approval of a social system from which they have received only the pits.

Her dislike of Alice I attributed to the obvious fact that Alice was everything Bella was not and wished to be. But when I cornered her alone one morning in the drawing room and challenged her on this, she shed tears which seemed to have little to do with envy.

"You have Mother and Percy all for you," she said bitterly as she dried her eyes. "Why must you drag me into it?"

"Mother doesn't strike me as so enthusiastic. She keeps telling me how young I am."

"She knows that nothing dampens ardor like too much parental approval. Don't all great lovers *want* to be star-crossed?"

I stared. "Do you mean that Mother affected coolness to *push* me at Alice?"

"Oh, it wasn't that deliberate on her part, of course not." Bella seemed impatient at my obtuseness. "Men can never understand women like Mother and Alice."

"Women like Mother and Alice! What on earth do you mean? Aren't *you* like Mother and Alice?"

"I hope not. I have no desire to push people around. Oh, that's putting it crudely, I know. They mean well, I'm sure. They want only the nicest things for you. It's just . . . well, if you must know, they don't have a very high opinion of men. They have to be always twitching the curtains and straightening the rug to keep the clumsy boobs from making a complete mess of the whole stage set."

"Stage set? What stage set?"

"That's what they think life is. It's certainly what they make of it, anyway. A pretty parlor comedy with a lot of witty lines and a sweet clinch at the final curtain."

"Well, I never!" I paused to evaluate this disagreeable concept. "But you have to admit Mother doesn't consider Percy a boob."

"No, but he's the son of an English nobleman, and she's an Anglophile. I've even heard her say that's why English upper-class women are so vapid. There's nothing for them to do; their husbands are perfect."

"And you suppose she expects Alice to take care of me and my crazy ideas?"

"Precisely."

I didn't like this. I didn't like it at all. "Do you imply they worked it out together?"

"No. Because they didn't have to. They understand each other instinctively."

But Bella still agreed to be one of Alice's bridesmaids at the large and splendid wedding that Mother was only too happy to give us. I resolved to say nothing to Alice about Bella's theory, but I certainly didn't forget it.

Alice was superlative on our honeymoon in Kenya; she was everything I could possibly have expected of her. She managed always to look sleek and well groomed, like those movie stars in later safari dramas, with every hair in place under her sun helmet and a light rifle slung smartly over her shoulder. In that heyday of the almighty dollar we had twenty bearers, and even a pleated skirt could be hand pressed for her at night. She also proved a fair shot, having taken lessons at a rifle range before we sailed, and her health in the worst heat was sturdier than my own. When she felled her first lion with a single shot in the head, she won the total approval of our not easily enthused white hunter. My only doubt was whether she was really enjoying herself. Was something being put on for my benefit? But then I have already, I note, used the analogy to an actress.

And what about myself? Wasn't *I* putting on a bit of a show for her? Had I not spent three hours to her one on that range on Long Island with a vision in mind of how fine I should look bringing down a charging cape buffalo at thirty yards? In the pursuit of pleasure the inner picture of oneself pursuing it may provide half the fun. And when I did bring down a magnificent bull with glorious horns, thundering across the veldt to trample me to dust, had I not, even with my eye on the sights and my finger on the trigger, seen myself as a hero? Why, it may be asked, did the man who had quaked all night in that shell hole at Verdun escape the claw of panic at such a moment? Because my life in the trenches would have been thrown away without reason or satisfaction, while in Kenya it would have been sacrificed to the joy of a fair duel.

Our months in Africa were followed by spring in a Florentine villa and summer on a chartered sailing yacht among the Greek islands. By fall we were established in a flat in Paris on the Rue Monsieur where our daughter Lisa was born. And now we settled down to amuse ourselves in the rootless world of postwar expatriates who were trying to find beauty in their own confused reactions to a Gallic culture which never confused the Gauls. Our new friends could not understand why the French were never "disillusioned," to use the catchword of the day. Because they had never had illusions, I used to answer. But then had we?

Alice and I provided a nightly asylum of good drinks and light music and pretentious talk for these unsettled souls. We had a nurse for Lisa and a cook and maid to care for the apartment. I spent my mornings writing or painting in a studio on the roof of our building; Alice took courses at the Sorbonne or sketched by the Seine. In the afternoon we walked our poodles or went to galleries, and in the evening, of course, there were the parties, where we were guests or hosts, usually the latter. Writers, artists, sexual deviants, alcoholics, reds, anarchists and just drifters filled our long living room and drank the inexhaustible booze. I had only one rule: everyone had to be out of the place by two in the morning. A certain regularity is essential to keep the demon ennui at bay.

For it had not taken me long to perceive that there was very little pleasure in this world of supposed pleasure seekers. People would disappear without explanation; it was often assumed they had just gone home. We had our suicides. Persons who are always talking about themselves are rarely happy, and egotism was the trademark of the crowd. It is true that we had among us some artists and writers of considerable talent, and one novelist of genius. But a drunken genius is only another drunk at a party.

No, if there was to be excitement for me in Paris, it had to be in what was produced, not in who was producing it. And that had to be true of myself as well; I had to work. I allotted four hours of each day to creation: two to my novel and two to my painting. That may not seem much, but I did a good deal of thinking about both in the other hours. Accomplishment in the arts is not only with the fingers. At least so I excused myself.

What was in all this for Alice? I was never sure. Her temper was remarkably equable. She never complained or seemed out of sorts; on the other hand, she never showed much enthusiasm for our friends or even for Paris. At parties she was cool and mildly detached, but she talked easily and well on most topics, with a sarcastic wit that people found attractive. Only with the baby was she really warm and loving. With me she was loyal, compliant, amused and amusing, but less than passionate. What bothered me most was that she somehow conveyed the impression of not finding France — or was it our life in France? — quite real.

My first and only novel, *Revelry by Night*, was composed in six months. It was only a couple of hundred pages, written in those simple declarative sentences which had become the style of the day. It told the story of a handsome and privileged young couple, very much like Alice and myself, who deemed themselves deeper of spirit and more adventurous than their hedonistic New York pals and escaped to Africa where the husband was killed by the fatal bite of a green mamba. My point was that even though he was seeking an unobtainable joy, he had still had a better life than those he had left behind in the playgrounds of his childhood. The book was actually published in monthly installments in a Paris-American magazine for new writing. The "genius" of our group was kind enough to say I had made a decent start.

Of course, the less talented were the sharper critics. Alice, after considerable urging on my part, related to me some comments not offered me directly.

"Well at least they could read me in print," I retorted, stung. "Which is more than I'll ever be able to do with their scribblings."

"What they can't bear is your facility. They don't see how a writer can be sober and well dressed and get to work in the morning."

"Exactly! They confuse dedication with alcoholism. Must all great writing be agonizing?"

"But doesn't even the public feel that? Didn't Trollope's

reputation take a dive when his fans discovered he wrote every morning from nine to twelve?"

"What rot it all is!" I suddenly found that I was actually angry. I must have put more of my heart into that novel than I had supposed. "What good is art, really? They say that in a godless world you can be saved by it. 'Redeemed,' I believe, is the fancy word. But *who* can be? You certainly can't be redeemed by somebody else's art, so it must be your own you're counting on. And presumably only great art can redeem, and how many great artists are there? Even Calvin would have saved more souls than *that*. So a fig for redemption by art!"

"Why don't you concentrate on your painting?" was Alice's patient suggestion.

My painting, I believe, was better than my writing, but it may also have been lacking in adventure. I had a preference for the early cubists, particularly Braque, before they began to specialize in deconstructed brown violins, and I did some quite nice geometrical landscapes, where the hills and trees, in somber greens and greys, were shaped like spheres and triangles. With Paris streets I was even more successful, and I was able to arrange a show in a small gallery in Montmartre with a large amount of alcohol for my *vernissage*. Picasso himself showed up and made a comment about one little picture which, with a twist or so, might almost have been construed as a compliment.

On the morning after my opening Alice paid a rare visit to my rooftop studio. Her countenance seemed rather drawn. Very firmly, she picked the canvas on which I was working off the easel and turned its back to me. I took a seat and waited patiently for her remonstrances as to the undue attention I might have paid to a certain blonde at the gallery party. Alice was not a jealous woman; it was the proprieties she cared about. My conduct had hardly been serious, and I anticipated a rapid pardon. But it turned out that she had no such trivia on her mind.

"What I'm about to say, Nat, is something I've been working out very carefully in my mind for several weeks now. So don't pooh-pooh it till you've given it proper thought." She paused. "I think I should tell you that I've talked to the only two friends we have over here who to my mind make any basic sense."

"Who are?"

"I don't want to tell you. It would put you off the point. Suffice it to say that they agree with me."

"About what?"

"About your having no real future as an artist. *Or* as a writer. Of fiction, anyway. Oh, we're not saying you don't do things well. You do. You even have an amazing flair for one with so little training. What you've accomplished already might be enough for a lot of people. But not for you. You'd never be content with that. Because you don't basically want to be an artist at all. You want to be the best artist. That is, you want the best of everything. You strike me as looking for some ultimate experience or test or joy or even agony . . . I don't know how to put it. But what I do know is you're never going to find it in Paris with a group of second- or even third-rate expatriates who kid themselves that life and art are to be found in drink and drugs and sex. Why, you're not even interested in those things!"

"Not in sex? Oh, Alice!"

"Well, with me perhaps."

I laughed. What else could the suddenly deflated do? "Darling, you know everything! A Gallic husband would leave you for that crack — unless he killed you first. But it's true. I *have* been faithful to thee, Cynara. After *my* fashion."

Alice shook her head to reject any jesting. "This is a time for absolute candor. If you've been faithful to me, it's because it's suited your book. The book you play everything by, yourself. And I've been willing to go along with you. I was even curious to see where you'd come out. But now I've seen it. You've come out nowhere."

Was I seeing that pale hard face for the first time? How could any woman — or man, for that matter — have kept up so fixed an appearance for so long? I think my primary reaction was one of admiration.

"Perhaps it is not too late, then, to start seeing things your way."

Her stare seemed to tremble into something more relaxed. But then a gleam of panic flickered in her eyes.

"Don't disarm me, Nat. I've screwed up my courage to say this, and I'm going to say it."

"Say it. Say it."

"I'm pregnant."

It was certainly news to take even me out of myself. I jumped up to embrace her. "Did you think I wouldn't be glad?"

"Oh, I knew you wouldn't mind. I'm sure you're anxious for a son. But what we have to do now is go home. And I'm afraid you're going to have to take a job. There'll be more expenses now, and you must quit spending capital."

I blinked. "How do you know I have been?"

"Percy and I have been corresponding. He knows all the family money matters. And he's lined up a job for you in Bogan & Steers. With a real future, he tells me."

I threw up my hands in a semi-serious surrender that would be the preface, I already sensed, of greater capitulations. "So I *shall* be selling bonds, after all."

"No, no, it's much more than that." Her voice was now

eager as she scented victory. "It'll be investing in new companies. All kinds of new businesses. Oh, Nat, my dear, you do everything well. Why not do well in making money for a while? I'll bet on you to be a millionaire in two years' time!"

6

I *did* become a millionaire; that was the funny thing. But not for long. Alice and I returned to New York, where Nat Junior was born seven months later. We moved into a charming little duplex on Park Avenue which Mother had bought for us.

That, of course, was Mother's way. She would never have settled a hundred thousand dollars on me, but she didn't hesitate to spend that or more for a flat. She loved to make lavish gifts in kind on even minor anniversaries, and Alice, knowing that Mother never remembered what she had given, would quietly convert some of them into hard cash. But this soon ceased to be necessary.

It did not take me long to find my place in Bogan & Steers. At first the partners accorded me the simple *bonhomie* which is the due of any limited and presumably silent partner — Percy had induced Mother to buy me a small share in the firm that handled her money. But when they found that I kept regular office hours, attended all firm lunches, listened carefully to the discussions and even asked an occasional intelligent question, they began to take me more seriously and to bring me into their projects.

Mines were the field I chose for my specialty, gold, silver, copper, I didn't care. I enjoyed the expeditions to wildernesses in Canada and our Northwest, to each of which I would always append a hunting or fishing trip. I loved the great cold menacing woods, the easy companionship of the camp life, the excavations, the sense of grasping riches from the rich earth, so much more romantic, so much more "real" even, than the swapping of commercial paper by hairy hands under the stare of etiolated faces in the gnome world of Wall Street.

Two of our mines, both in Canada, proved promising; our stock offerings were oversubscribed. Alice and I expanded our style of living. We had a cottage in Maine now for the summer, and another for weekends near Mother on Long Island; I had a forty-foot sailboat and a Hispano-Suiza. And we entertained as we had in Paris, although a much more conservative crowd. Yet nothing seemed to close the gap that had opened between us at our first serious confrontation. I even had the feeling that Alice didn't really want to close it.

One night, as we were having a final drink after the last guest had left, she put this to me.

"Let me ask you something, Nat. Were you feeling tonight that our guests weren't quite real?"

"What on earth do you mean?"

"Well, I was watching you as you circled the room. You talked to everyone. You saw that their drinks were refilled. In fact, you were the perfect host, as always. Yet I found myself wondering if you were really there."

"I might have been thinking about my gold mine. Don't we all daydream? Isn't that what psychiatrists call free association?"

"But I mean something more than that. Could you be one of those people who believe that everything they see, the whole universe in fact, is simply a product of their imagination?"

"Maybe I'm just the product of *yours*."

"I wonder if mine wouldn't have produced something more different."

"Alice! Spare my feelings, please."

"I mean, wouldn't it have produced someone who loved me?" At which she burst into tears.

There was no point talking to Alice when she got like that. We had been drawing apart steadily, although she claimed we had never been together. What can you do with a woman who is always insisting on the need of some kind of togetherness that is probably obtainable only by persons of the dullest imagination? Perhaps she thought it might be obtainable with Tommy Steers, the rugged thickset perennial bachelor who was considered the genius of our firm and whose mind, so far as I could make out, was occupied exclusively by the money market and by Alice. I used to twit her about his silent canine adoration. He came to all our parties and rarely took his eyes off her.

"Do me the favor of not pretending to be jealous" was her curt answer to one of my cracks. "If I keep Tommy as a pet, it's to remind myself that I'm still a woman."

Our marriage ended with the crash of 1929. It was the end of my mining companies and their rashly overextended financing. I had put everything I had into them; all was lost. Yet I found myself intrigued by the "twilight of the gods" atmosphere of Wall Street, the frank admission by so many that there was no life apart from new riches, the "defenestrations." Although I did not share the despair, I was interested to be one of the losers. I told Alice that for the first time in my life I felt a cognate part of a considerable section of humanity. She did not see this as significant. A future of only moderate means appalled her.

"Well, after all, we're not destitute," I observed.

"I'd like to know why not."

"Mother will let us move in with her in Locust Valley. Bella has that whole wing to herself. She'll be glad to share it, and anyway, she dotes on the children. And Percy says Ma will pick up the school bills."

"But they'll be different schools!"

"What's wrong with that? They'll be just as good. Mother's lost too much money herself to support us here. Doubling up, we can get by."

"Doubling up! You mean living on your mother's charity. I have to give up my home and independence, and Lisa the school she loves and little Nat his kindergarten!"

"But, Alice dear, most people are much worse off. How many have parents who can take them in?"

"You've always counted on your mother, haven't you?"

"Well, she was always there to count on, wasn't she? It's a blessing she only lost half her fortune."

"While your father lost *all* of his. Was that the real reason you hated him?"

"Alice, don't be vulgar. It doesn't become you."

"You were always sneering about his blinding himself to reality! But wasn't the poor man working his head off to save a business for all the mill hands who depended on it? And wasn't he trying to make a man of you and not the dressy dilettante your mother preferred? You never tired of telling me that your father stood for dullness and death and your mother for life and amusement. But what is she now but an old society gadabout who's ruined a daughter and spoiled a son rotten?"

"Was it spoiling me to do everything in her power to promote our marriage?"

"She didn't at first. She thought we were too young. But

then it occurred to her that maybe I'd be able to straighten out the mess that even she could see she'd made of you. Only it was too late."

My curiosity overcame my anger. "Did you and she discuss that?"

"Yes! She had just enough common sense to realize that her life as a woman wouldn't do for a man. She thought I might wean you in time from your silly ideas."

"Well, you came pretty close. If it hadn't been for the Depression, you might even have won out. After all, you made me make money."

"But could I make you save it? Did it ever cross your mind, while you were raking it in, to set up a trust for me and the children? Even a small bread-and-butter one? Oh, no! You put every penny you didn't blow on fancy cars and clothes back into those damn mines. And now you have the gall to boast about your shared experience! Prince Nathaniel has joined the human race at last!"

"Alice! Now you *are* vulgar."

"And it reminds you of my father's unpaid bridge debts, doesn't it? Well, let me tell you something even more vulgar. I'm leaving you. I'm going to divorce you and marry Tommy!"

The news hardly came as a blow. It was even rather a relief. The prospect of sharing a house with Alice and Mother was not an agreeable one. I knew that Tommy had weathered the crash and would be a good stepfather. Why not make use of him? Alice, turned hopelessly sour, was little loss, and I doubted that she would interfere with my visiting the children. And as to settlements, what had I to settle?

Does what I have just written sound hard and selfish? But that in my opinion is the inevitable result of a man's honest effort to tell the truth about himself. Deep down, we are all pretty much the same. We hate to face our real natures, so we drop over the scene of our theatricals a thick scrim of sentimentality. Alice and I had been strongly attracted to each other, but neither would have wed the other without a condition met. I had obtained her assurance that she would be my partner in the quest for the good life (as I defined it), and she had satisfied herself and her parents that I was financially sound. Now each had failed the other. She had lost her interest in the good life, and I had lost my money. A divorce was the only fair and rational solution.

7 For the next few years I lived with Mother and Percy. They made everything beautifully pleasant. I had almost a private house in the wing I shared with Bella, and I was urged to give my own parties in the big dining room on the frequent weekends when the Maxwells were visiting friends. Percy arranged that I should have an ample allowance for my personal expenses, which I accepted without demur. Why not? Was he not living on Mother too?

I recalled what Alice had suggested to me long before: that I take up chess which one could play forever. I did, and bridge too, and golf, and became expert at all three. I was easily the most popular "extra man" on the north shore. As Percy and Mother grew older, I took over more and more of the running of the estate; we won prizes for the garden and for the Black Angus raised on the farm.

I had no interest in marrying again. In the local society

there were plenty of bored and beautiful wives with whom I could enjoy discreet affairs, except where discretion was not necessary. And as Tommy and Alice had moved to nearby Glen Cove, I was able to see my children on a regular basis and had the satisfaction of rebutting to them some of their stepfather's stuffier principles.

And so life passed, surely not wasted, but also lacking in the best that I was still convinced it had to offer to the discriminating seeker. The disillusionment that I can see now was all along inevitable had to await an event that it shames me even now to record.

One of my economies in managing the estate for Mother and Percy was to convert the superintendent's cottage (no longer needed as I was now essentially that), a charming red brick miniature manor house in the Queen Anne style, to a rentable residence for some attractive young couple who would fit in with our neighborhood and maybe help to fill out a bridge table on Saturday nights. And just such a pair did I find in the Danny Gateses, who were soon taken to the bosom not only of my family, but of the whole community of my friends.

They were considerably the youngest of my group, both being still under thirty, but they seemed blithely unconscious of age, and Danny proclaimed to all that he had lost his heart to my mother. He was florid, blond and muscular, with standard American good looks which he might one day lose to fat; he played excellent golf and tennis, and the noisy, even rather vulgar, but still infectious laugh with which he greeted the jokes of his seniors endeared him greatly to them. He worked for a brokerage house in the city, but his gleaming Lincoln Zephyr, his bright sport jackets and his membership in many clubs bespoke independent means.

Alfreda Gates was less conspicuous but of rarer quality than her husband. If quieter, she had greater self-assurance.

Her pretty heart-shaped face and cute curly brown hair had not at first prepared me for the deeper enchantment of her wide-apart and wide eyes of palest blue which met one's own with a mildly questioning air that seemed to imply the possibility of any number of relationships. I know that makes her sound like a flirt, but she wasn't. It was rather that she saw no reason to conceal her awareness of the obvious fact that every meeting of two human beings contains a multitude of potential futures. She and Danny had a beautiful four-year-old son on whom they properly doted.

I soon became a favorite of both Gateses. Indeed, they almost vied with each other for my attention. Danny, who professed a strong if not always discriminating love of the arts, sought my advice in his reading list and flattered me by borrowing a copy of my old novel and declaring it the equal of Fitzgerald. Alfreda got me to give her putting lessons on the lawn, consulted me in questions of decorating the cottage and generally treated me as the *arbiter elegantiarum* of the community. Of course, I fell in love with her, but I did not know at first how deeply.

It was on weekday evenings, when she would sometimes call, just before dinner, to ask me to come over and take pot luck with them, that I became most intimate with the Gateses. There was little that Danny, after a few drinks, was reluctant to discuss.

"Alfy and I are very passionate persons. We make wonderful love together and never seem to tire of each other. But I don't think I could ever be a jealous spouse. If she were to hanker for a bit of variety, if it were ever to mean *that* much to her to go off on a toot with no questions asked, I think I could see my way to accepting it. So long as she didn't make a public ass of me."

Alfreda's laugh had a bit of a bite in it. "Perhaps you'd like to watch me through a hole in the wall, the way you did in that Paris brothel in your good old bachelor days. What a treat! Did you ever go to places like that, Nat?"

"I never had to buy my love. Much less watch it."

"There's one for you, Danny boy!"

But Danny's laugh was unabashed. "That was when I was only eighteen. When did it first happen to you, Nat?"

I told him the story of how Grandpa had initiated me; he listened intently.

"Why do they call Paris the City of Light?" Alfreda mused. "Darkness would seem the better word. Darkness, anyway, would describe *my* initiation. We poor girls have a messy time meeting up with the 'facts.' "

"I thought I'd been a passable instructor."

Alfreda turned to me with another of her laughs. "He prides himself on being such a sexual liberal! But he's still enough of a rutting bull to want to think of himself as my first."

"You *know* I was, sweetheart. I never bought that tale of you and your cousin Bob in the cow barn at age twelve."

"But it still nags you!"

"Not a bit of it. I leave posthumous jealousy to the inky paw of Mister Proust."

These conversations were upsetting to me. The sexual attraction between these two young animals was very evidently strong, and I found its necessary exclusion of myself painful. I was beginning to realize that I was suffering from what is supposed to be the well-deserved fate of men who have dallied too long with love. When it grips them at last, particularly in middle age, its grasp may be like the fatal one of the bronze Venus in the Mérimée tale. My desire to possess the voluptuous Alfreda threatened to make rubble of my long-cultivated equanimity, and I seized greedily on the idea that her husband might tolerate an affair. But had I any reason to suppose that if the lovely lady should decide to play, her choice of partner would alight on one so much her senior?

There came a night, however, when it struck me that all might not be quite as well between them as I had surmised. An hour after the three of us had dined, Danny yawned and announced he was going to bed. Alfreda said she would sit up for another drink with me.

"Well, I know I'm safe in leaving you even with such a randy old goat as Nat," Danny observed, giving me a crude wink as he moved to the stair. "It's that time of the month, my friend."

Alfreda was suddenly irate. "Why don't you ask Nat to spend the night in our bedroom? Are we to have *no* private life?"

"Oh, Nat understands."

"Of course Nat understands. Any idiot would understand you. *I'm* the one who's beginning not to understand. What *is* this compulsion of yours to leave the bathroom door open?"

"Somebody got out of bed on the wrong side this morning."

"And maybe she won't get back into it!"

"Good *night*, Alfy." Danny now turned to make me a formal bow. "I leave you to the company of this charmingly good-tempered lady."

Alone with me, Alfreda poured herself a strong drink and settled back on the sofa.

"I don't know what gets into Danny. He's always trying to impress his elders and betters with how smart he is, or what a great athlete he is, or, like tonight, how titillatingly shocking he can be."

"But at least he succeeds. All the older people dote on him."

"I sometimes think he's looking for the parents he never

had. He was an adopted child, you know. And he's always playing the cute little boy, the smartest kid on the block, the sexy impudent teenager, a crude bid for amused adult attention." She sighed. "I can see why some women prefer older men."

"Like me, I hope."

She didn't pick this up. "Oh, I don't say I'm one of them. Though I may get there yet." She had been talking half to herself, but now she leaned over to touch my hand. "You're wonderfully understanding, Nat. Danny and I both really love you."

"Both?"

"Well, I don't suppose Danny's is an unnatural lust, though I sometimes wonder. He *does* go on about you."

I dared now to press this further. "Yours anyway is quite normal. And perfectly safe, too."

"Safe?"

"From Danny's jealousy. He says he hasn't any."

"I wonder if that's true." I saw I had lost my lead in her new interest. "He might take an infidelity on my part as a happy license to go romping himself. I question if any man should marry before forty."

"In that case I've been ready for three years. Will you be my bride, Alfreda?"

She matched her smile to mine. "If you'd met me five years ago, Nat!" But then she caught something else in my expression. "Maybe Danny's right. Maybe you *are* a randy old goat. Good night, Nat, dear!"

Was I an ass to take encouragement from her bantering tone? Anyway, I promptly took my leave.

Danny and I went out riding early the next morning which was a Sunday. He was beginning to get on my nerves. It was not enough that he had everything I wanted, youth and a beautiful wife to share it with; he had to add the luxury of cheap melancholy.

"Do you know who I'd like to be?" He reined up his horse to emphasize the gravity of his question. "And someone I never will be?"

"Who?"

"You, Nat."

I rode on, disgusted. "Me! My God, man, don't you know a failure when you see one?"

"On the contrary, I see a resounding success."

"But what the hell have I ever done?"

"It's not what you've done, though in fact you've done everything, far more than I could ever dream of accomplishing. You've written, you've painted, you've made a fortune and lost it. But it's what you *are* that I envy. You *live* so beautifully. You fill every dull moment of life with a high style."

I simply couldn't bring myself to answer him, so I rode ahead, letting my back signify that the discussion was closed. Was he mocking me? Not consciously, of course. He hadn't the wit for that. But had I not, in creating his presence in the remodeled superintendent's cottage, been responsible for my own punishment in this caricature of Nat Chisolm in middle life? He envied *me!* When I would have made him a willing present of all I had or was in return for a single night with his wife!

Impatience was making me reckless. What anyway did I owe to so deluded a fool as Danny? Surely his wife deserved something better after her years with him. I was determined that she should know my feeling, regardless of what her response might be, and I picked a moment when neither of us could properly raise our voices or even much alter our facial expressions. It was at one of Mother's big dinner par-

ties when Alfreda and I were seated together (at my planning) in the middle of the long table before the principal
figure of the elaborate silver centerpiece: a Venus rising on
her shell from waters of papier-mâché.

My voice was matter-of-fact. "You must know by now
that I love you."

Her nod was of the slightest, her pause reflective. "I suppose you think you do."

"That's what people have always said about me. But
you're the first one to be wrong. Because you're the first
woman I've ever loved. Really loved." It was such a relief to
be saying it, actually uttering those words to her, that I
wanted to laugh in sheer pleasure. "Venus is smiling at me.
She didn't think I'd have the nerve. But surely she ap-
proves."

"Don't be too sure."

"Tell me. Do I have the smallest chance?"

"Of what?"

"Of marrying you. Of living with you. Of having an affair
with you. Of kissing you. Oh, I'm a starving beggar. I'll take
any crumb."

Her next pause was almost judicial. "I might let you kiss
me. Beyond that, deponent sayeth not."

"A kiss is all I ask."

"Your mother's looking at us. It's time to switch."

Mother was indeed looking at us, but whether as a signal
to talk to our other table neighbors or as a reproof of our
intimacy, I couldn't be sure. How did she always know?
Alfreda turned to the man on her other side and I to the lady
on mine, but I must have been a wretched dinner partner,
for my heart was pounding in such a way that I could neither
talk nor listen. All I could think of was that that promised
kiss might open up at last a world I had always dreamed
would be mine.

But I was never to have it. Not even on the cheek. The next morning Mother sent for me to her room, where she was finishing the breakfast she always had in bed.

"There's a little matter of business to discuss." By placing her fingers on the handles of her tray she indicated that I was to remove it, which I at once did. "Percy and I have agreed that we should promote Jim Cain to be superintendent of the place. We both think you're doing too much for us. And if we do that, we'll be needing the Gates cottage back. Their year is almost up. Will you give them the necessary notice?"

I placed her tray on a table, keeping my back to her. "You really want to *evict* the Gateses?"

"They won't mind. They want a bigger place anyway. Danny's told me so. And they'll have to have one if they have another child."

"*Are* they having another child?"

"I haven't the least idea. But I assume they want to have more than one."

I noted the guarded half-smile which Mother always used when she apprehended danger. "Mother, what are you trying to tell me?"

"That I want them off this place." The smile had vanished. "For their sakes. And for ours."

"Do you think I'm having an affair with Alfreda?"

"I don't know. *Are* you?"

"No."

After a silence she pursued: "Well, if that's the case, let's by all means keep it that way. Let's remove temptation as far as we can. It won't be very far, but it's better than right next door."

"Let me tell you something, Mother. With me this is really serious. More so than anything that has ever happened to me. I want to marry Alfreda."

But Mother was prepared for this, too. Her tone was cold, as it could be when her basic conventionality took hold of her will. "It's a pity, then, that she's already married."

"She could get a divorce."

"Yes, but *would* she?"

What did Mother know? I recalled how unconscionably long the ladies had been away from us after dinner the night before. She *could* have taken Alfreda to her bedroom for a warning chat. "Mother, have you *talked* to Alfreda?"

"And if I had, do you know what I would have told her? That if she were ever tempted to leave that fine young husband of hers for a jaded middle-aged pleasure seeker, she'd be a sorry fool!"

I could hardly believe she had said it! Had she been storing her maternal power for years to expend it all in one fatal blow? I sank on my knees by her bed and covered my face with my hands.

"I didn't know you could be so murderous," I murmured.

"I can do anything, thank God, when it comes to saving my boy from an act of folly." She had sat forward, and I could feel her fingers in my hair. "You're too kind a man to break up a young family like that. This is only a moment of madness, as you will see in a brief time."

"But isn't it too late, Mother?" I implored her, as if she were some kind of grim judge with my life in her hands. "Isn't Alfreda already disillusioned with her husband? Isn't she bound to leave him for another man? And mightn't it be an even worse one than me?"

"Stuff and nonsense. You don't know young brides. The most loving of them have moments when they're ready to bolt. I *know*. That is just the time when they need steadying. It's quite possible for a young woman to be so exasperated with the silly values of a fatuous spouse that she's tempted to *tromper* him with the very man he admires!"

So now I knew. I got up and walked to the window from which I could just make out the dormer of the Gateses' cottage. I put together how skillfully Mother must have got the story out of Alfreda and doused any incipient feeling on the girl's part with the shower of her common sense. And wasn't she right? Alfreda *was* better off with a Danny, whose body she would continue to enjoy and whose disquisitions she would learn not to hear. One night of love with him would probably eradicate the memory of her flirtation with me. I may have owed what small attention I had received to the monthly period Danny had been vulgar enough to mention.

"And what do I do now?"

"Why, I think, my dear son, that everything points to a nice long trip. Hadn't you better take advantage of the time before that crazy man, Hitler, sets the whole world on fire again?"

8 I decided to take up my stepbrother on a long-standing invitation to visit him in Nairobi. Alistair Maxwell, despite his manipulation of an artificial leg so agile as almost to conceal his handicap, had not married but had settled, after the war, in Kenya where for years he had successfully conducted hunting safaris for rich Americans and Britons. He was a tall, cool, self-contained and satiric fellow who treated the nabobs with reserved and at times even acerbic good manners, envying no man and admiring few, calm in crisis and, needless to say, a perfect shot. He and I had always hit it off, and he took me out on a lion hunt, just the two of us

with two bearers. My marksmanship was now good enough for even his standards, and at night outside our tent we would drink plentiful whiskey, smoke and discuss the folly and futility of a world headed straight for another global conflict.

"But who am I to point the finger?" I asked him one night. "Am I doing anything even as harmless as fiddling while Rome burns? No, I'm killing beasts a thousand times nobler than my own silly self. Oh, I'm sorry, Alistair," I added when I felt the chill of his nonresponse. "You must be so sick of that kind of Yankee self-flagellation. It surely doesn't keep us from going right on killing."

"I've noticed that too. But is the lion any nobler than you? Would you kill your cubs to bring your mate into heat? Massacre your posterity for a quicker screw? *He* would. And what about her? Tickled pink to swap the nursery for the double bed!"

"But that's their nature, Alistair!"

"And it's ours to hunt them."

"But is it the *better* part of our nature?"

Alistair yawned. "I daresay it's the better part of mine. But if you really want to be noble and still hunt, there's a rogue elephant that's been marauding the farms in this neighborhood. He may even have killed a woman who's been missing for some days now. The local yokels would be mighty grateful if we knocked him off. How's that for eating your cake and having it too?"

I jumped to my feet. "But that's a great idea! Like the knights-errant of old, scouring the countryside to find the wicked dragon that's wasting the land. The hunt with a high goal. Do you realize, Alistair, you may have hit on the ultimate pleasure? Can we go after it tomorrow?"

"If I can find the 'noble' beast. We'll set out at dawn. And if you'll take my advice, no more whiskey tonight. Old rogues can be very nasty. And very sly."

That night I slept as soundly as if I had solved the problems of a lifetime. We set out at six, Alistair at the wheel of our small truck. He steered with his left hand, holding in his right the field glasses with which he scanned the horizon. Occasionally he would stop to study some distant object. But in only an hour's time he turned off the motor and pointed silently to a green marshy spot in the middle of the brown veldt that separated us from a chain of small rocky hills. A bull elephant was half concealed in the rushes on which it was feeding; only its mountainous black back and slowly wagging ears were visible.

Dropping my glasses, I gazed about to familiarize myself with the scene of our approaching encounter. The lower part of a pale lavender sky was slit by a long thin line of haze. Beyond the marsh, at the foot of the hills, were dozens of black dots, a herd of grazing wildebeest. Nearer the car, at a hundred yards, were three zebra and a giraffe.

"He's downwind," Alistair murmured. "We should be in shooting distance before he spots us." His hand was on the door handle. "Walk slowly."

"I want to go alone."

"Don't be a fool, man. If you miss and he charges, you'll need a backup."

"I won't miss. Leave it to me. Please."

Alistair, who knew all about Americans and their fetish of manhood, shrugged. "All right, only at least I'll get out of the car."

I nodded. "But please stay back."

I stepped carefully out of the truck and, unslinging my rifle, started my wary approach. As the black back swelled to my vision, I was pleased to confirm its unusual size. When the bull raised his head in an act of swallowing, I noted that the curled tusks were long and fine. Half hypnotized, I was barely conscious of using the muscles in my legs. The rogue seemed to be drawing me like a magnet. Suddenly he lifted his trunk. Had he scented me? I froze, as in a game of statues. But then he resumed his feeding with a massive, majestical indifference to anything in the world but his own appetite.

He was more than a beast, even a noble beast, to me now. My Moby Dick, if you will. As seemingly black as the whale was albino. And he was evil, too, appallingly evil, as joy-destroying as the iron mills of Troy which had crushed the life out of my misguided father or the guns of Verdun that felled a generation of golden lads.

But he must have his chance.

"Hey!" I called to him, at perhaps seventy yards.

And now, with a heavy turning and thrashing, he heaved himself out of the rushes and faced me, the great ears flapping, as wondrously fierce as some impossible monster in a wild dream.

I took aim and held my fire until the charging fury was only twenty yards away and then gently pressed the trigger. My first shot stopped him, and I fancied he looked stunned, surprised. My immediate second felled him, and I heard Alistair's congratulatory whistle.

It was the happiest moment of my life.

Leaving Kenya, I went home via Vienna where Mother and Percy were staying. Percy's sister was married to an Austrian baron, Otto von Stahr, and they wanted to see how she and her family were faring after the Anschluss. The Nazis were inclined to favor the nobility, but one of their sons had publicly opposed the forced union of the two nations and

had been able to escape from Austria only through the dip-
lomatic wire-pulling of his uncle. Percy had been long re-
tired from the foreign service, but he was still called upon
for various discreet missions, and I had little doubt that he
was now engaged in some kind of private investigation for
the British government. He certainly showed himself very
well informed on German-Austrian relations when I dined
with him and Mother in their suite at the Sacher.

Whatever Percy may have been doing for the Foreign Office, he was certainly no appeaser, and he spoke with fervent
admiration of the warning role now played by his friend
Winston Churchill. When I protested that the whole mess
in Europe was the result of the vicious peace at Versailles
and that England could not expect us a second time to save
an empire most of which she ought to give up anyway,
Mother cried out at what she called my ostrich-like isolation-
ism.

"That's not fair, Ma. All I'm saying is that if Britain and
France hadn't worked themselves into such a lather of hate
in the last war and had compromised earlier on a sensible
peace, they'd now be dealing with Hohenzollerns and not
Hitlers. Why should Americans pay for their folly?"

"The Kaiser was certainly better than the Führer," Percy
conceded. "And no doubt some of those Belgian horror stories were exaggerated. I was never one to buy toilet paper
decorated with the likeness of Wilhelm II. But none of that
is now in question, Nat. The war that is surely coming has
little to do with empires and markets and nineteenth-century
ideologies. Oh, they're mixed up in it, of course. But the
real point is that this time we seem to be up against the devil
himself."

"Aren't you being rather dramatic?" I asked. "Isn't Herr
Hitler just another brute?"

But Percy shook his head. "Men of good will tend to believe that there must always be two sides to every question. Especially in international disputes. That is what the Nazis are counting on. That the world will not see that there is nothing on their side at all. That they are evil. Evil incarnate."

"Percy!" I exclaimed. "You sound like a T. S. Eliot poem. And I've always thought of you as the coolest of realists. What has happened to you?"

"Hitler has happened to me. I'll be glad to show you some reports I have when we get home."

"Well, so long as you don't make *me* read them!" Mother protested. "I can't bear tales of torture and killing."

"Then these indeed are not for you, my dear. But Nat is made of tougher stuff. I have no doubt he'll find them most convincing."

"You got me into one war, Percy," I reproached him, but with a grin. "I forewarn you, you're going to have to be *very* convincing to get me into another."

"Well, you have always been a student of pleasure, my boy. And one of the most searching and intelligent ones at that. You may be relieved to learn that the Nazis have left us one pleasure."

"And what is that?"

"Killing them! Or at least as many as we can."

His smile had vanished. But not mine. "You'll wait for a war, I hope."

"I shan't have to wait long."

I laughed. "Then a Nazi can be my rogue elephant!"

"What on earth do you mean by that?"

I told him.

🙚🙚🙚

9 When Britain declared war on Germany, only a year later, I asked Percy if he would help me to obtain a commission in the British army. I had spoken to no one else about my project, particularly not Mother. It was like him to manifest no surprise.

He had given me those intelligence reports of Nazi atrocities in the concentration camps. But to tell the truth, I had only glanced through them. It had not taken many pages to convince me that here at last was game that it would be a joy as well as a sport to kill. Nor did it make a difference that I might very well be killed myself. All that I feared was that if I should read too many of his reports, I might find the atrocities simply another chapter in the endless saga of man's brutality to man. Hitler to me had to be more than another rogue elephant. He had to be what I had been looking for all my life.

I had tried the pleasures of art, of finance, of love and of sport and had found plentiful rewards, but not the highest. Of course, a man is limited by his own capabilities. The exquisite delights of the greatest artists, lovers or magnates were not open to me. I had made do well enough — better than many — with what talents I possessed. And in sports I had attained a somewhat higher rank, though in sports the joy derived, even for the champions, may be more limited. Religion was closed to me, for I had no faith. And good works bored me. That was simply a fact I had to face. Some may say I faced it too well. There remained the field of domesticity, but after my divorce the children were always much more Alice's than mine.

As I looked back on the recent years when I lived with

Mother and Percy, it was a simple matter to deduce from them that pleasure is vitiated by total selfishness. I had lived exclusively for myself, and the staining of my character had stained my enjoyment of life. In war then, in a *good* war, I might unite pleasure with the satisfaction of being a straw in the broom that cleansed the world. I really did not see that I had any alternative but to get into it.

Percy owed it to Mother, I supposed, to put up at least a formal protest.

"But my dear boy — for to me you will be always that — it was only a matter of months ago in Vienna that you told me it wasn't the job of every American generation to pull Britain's chestnuts out of the fire."

"And maybe it isn't. I'm talking about *my* job. *You're* the one who convinced me, after all. You even told me it would be fun to kill Germans. So why shouldn't I have a fine time?"

"I must say, my dear fellow, it does seem a bit rough that millions must die to bring you this diversion."

"But I never wanted the war! I'm simply taking advantage of it now it's here. Is that wrong?"

"I suppose not." He sighed. "And I suppose, as a Britisher, I should be grateful, so long as we must fight, that anyone should relish of it. Yes, I daresay I can fit you up with something. You certainly look in first-class physical shape even if you're . . . how old?"

"Forty-five. Forty by candlelight. And I was commissioned a second looey in 1918. I've stayed in our reserve and done all the required training. And don't forget I saw the front."

"I shan't. But not a word of this to your ma before she has to know. The application may take some time and a bit of doing."

"And I have a project for the meanwhile. I'm going to

write the story of my idle life and leave it with you. Not to be read unless I don't return. Which I don't expect to. Which I'm not even sure I really want to."

"What nonsense, old boy. You survived the second battle of Verdun and that rogue elephant in Kenya. Not to mention the spills of polo and the bistros of Paris. Men like you make old bones."

"But not if they tempt fate too hard, as I fully intend to do."

We were in the library of the Long Island house, he and I alone after a dinner with Mother. He put down his liqueur glass and eyed it gloomily. "Dear boy, are you so unhappy?"

"Not at all. I've never been happier. As you will see when you read my story."

He shook his head doubtfully, as if he would never be able to make me out. "Will it be in the form of a memoir?"

"Maybe in the form of a novel. With an 'I' character who reconstructs dialogue he could never have remembered so exactly. The self-knowing narrator Henry James so much disapproved of. For who would have written his own life that way? Well, sir, Nat Chisolm would have!"

Percy smiled. "But if I do get to read it, he won't have known how it ended."

"Oh, he has a good idea."

But I had not meant to depress dear old Percy, and I challenged him now to a game of chess. I was and am perfectly willing to survive the conflict, provided it ends in victory, which at this point, considering German air power alone, is at least problematical. But I cannot help wondering where the aging bear I should then be would look for honey in the arid gardens of a postwar world. Maybe it is better that things should turn out for Nathaniel Chisolm as I suspect they shall.

The Realist
❦ ❦ ❦ ❦

1

My daughter Ellen has provoked me into writing this memoir. Her son Mark has just taken off for Sweden to escape the draft which might have sent him to fight in Vietnam. My husband was strongly of the opinion that the boy should have stayed and gone to jail if necessary, that he owed a duty to his country to take a stand, one way or the other, on the issue of the war. Ernest, at seventy-six, nine years my senior, is neither a dove nor a hawk, but he is always very strong on morals and holds that a man should stand up to be counted. This makes Ellen furious. She calls her father an antediluvian puritan who has lost all touch with the real issues of 1966. And she thinks I'm even worse for not openly disagreeing with him. For she insists on classifying me as typical of a female generation that deferred to the male in every respect but the adornment of their person and the decoration of their home.

"I almost envy you, really, Ma. You and your kind must have been the last people on earth to have no doubts. No real doubts. So long as you could lunch every day with your pals at the Murray Hill Club and summer in Northeast Harbor, you could leave all the big decisions to 'downtown' and to a country which had to be yours, right or wrong. Because it never crossed your mind that it could be wrong. Any more than it ever occurred to you that you might have brought your daughter up to face *some* changes in the world."

Ellen has been very sour since Frank left her two years ago for a woman half his age. I remember sitting with a group of young mothers at my club who were discussing at what age children were at their most difficult: four, six, eight, ten? I murmured: "Wait till they're fifty." Ellen is not fifty yet, but she's getting there. And although she insists on seeing my generation as the source of all the problems of her own, I don't give hers such great marks. She and her friends like to talk about how much more they've done with their lives, yet precious few of them have had professions or even jobs. Their *daughters* are preparing themselves for careers, but I don't give the parents all the credit for that. Ellen and *her* kind, in my book, have fallen between two stools. They haven't been the social leaders that my friends have been, nor the "men" their daughters will be. They really haven't been anything much, though I can't say that. Except in this memoir. Because I shan't know till it's finished whether or not I will show it to anyone.

I am talking now of a particular world, a small one. All particular worlds are small. It is easy to knock the *haute bourgeoisie* of Manhattan Island in the nineteen twenties and thirties — hardly anyone defends it — but how will our critics themselves look a few hundred years from now? "What?" our descendants may cry. "They put people in prisons! They ate flesh! They let stupid parents raise their own children! They bowed to the rule of idiotic majorities! What barbarians!"

Ellen loves to harp on the Murray Hill Club. Of course, it is no longer on Murray Hill, but on Madison Avenue and Seventieth Street, a fine, excellently equipped and well-appointed edifice built under my presidency in 1939. It surprises some of my granddaughters' friends that so "swank" a building should be a women's club. I tell them that it dates from the days when women *ran* New York, at least my part of town.

Ellen could never see this. She has always called the club a "refuge from reality" and describes my friends as a gaggle of plain, middle-aged or elderly females all talking at once about nothing. She hasn't the imagination to perceive that they constituted a force which used to control a surprising number of urban institutions in its time, not only some of the great charitable ones, but the private schools, the dancing classes and subscription parties, the whole social paraphernalia of raising the young of the dominant economic class of the city. Didn't someone have to do it? The men never would have. "But all that's over, Ma. You're talking about the dark ages!" But it wasn't over in *my* day, and should I have lived my life as if the future had been *then?* Should I have studied law and slaved in a firm that would never have considered making me a partner? Or should I, as I did, have taken up the really very interesting opportunities which then existed for the wives of the men downtown?

Ellen gets quite nasty when I use this argument, and implies that my friends overdid the power play, if that was what it was, that they even forgot they were women, and she passes some harsh judgments on the physical appearance of some of the prominent members of my club. I feel like telling her that they at least have managed to hold on to their husbands. It is true that many of them have ceased to be much concerned with sex; Ernest and I discontinued intimate relations more than twenty years ago by mutual consent, partly because of his arthritis. Certainly neither of us has since been unfaithful. Ellen says that none of my women friends has ever really tried to please a man. Well, we don't smirk and waggle our hips, if that's what she means! There's such a thing as mutual love and respect. And such a thing as human dignity.

Perhaps it could be said that in a world obsessed with sex the club *was* a refuge. The admission of men would have been fatal to the peculiar freedom of the atmosphere. Young men find it difficult to divorce themselves from the idea of at least potentially physical relations with women, even in casual chat, and older men, if freer of this (and that's not always the case!), tend to become garrulous and self-centered. Women together, after a certain age, are more capable of the truest friendship, and out of such friendships and the working together of our club members many fine things have resulted.

And having got *that* off my mind, I may now proceed to the episode which taught me how to deal with the men of *my* era.

2 Most people I have known have believed their childhood to have been unhappy. This is sometimes hard to be credited by observers blinded by the vision of privileges which had not been theirs to enjoy. The world into which I was born in 1900 was one which contained many servants and horses and fussy French interiors, and a great deal of bad art and rich food, but to me it was a world where a girl was supposed to be beautiful, and I was plain. I grew up flat-chested and skinny, with a brown oval face that defied the art of makeup, a strong nose and dull brown hair that was difficult to set. I had good eyes, however, grey-green pensive eyes. Lord knows I gazed at them often enough in my bedroom mirror.

"We can only hope that Alida's story will be that of Mr. Andersen's duckling," I overheard my father tell my mother. Or was it overheard? Daddy, very handsome himself and very conscious of it, with eagle eyes and a fine strong Roman nose, never much cared who might be listening. Whatever observation he might be making had to be worth more than children's tattle at the family board.

Herman Vermeule takes some explaining. In pre–World War I New York, the husbands, at least in *his* world, were usually so engrossed in moneymaking that they left the spending of it (and all the power which that entailed) to wives only too happy to pick up the challenge. When, however, the husband did not happen to be a breadwinner but the heir of one, domestic relations could take a very different turn. My father, if of esteemed but impoverished Dutch colonial stock on the paternal side, was also the grandson, on his mother's, of an odoriferous market manipulator, the notorious Cyrus Oates. Daddy had had to divide with many siblings and cousins the ill-gotten gains of that old pirate, but his share had still been enough, given his easy habit of never distinguishing between principal and income, to maintain hospitable mansions in town and country and equip his family with mounts for the fox hunting that he loved more than life itself. And so it was that he could afford (at least for *his* lifetime) to look for his models, not south to Wall Street but east, finding his chosen one in the gruff, barking English peer before whom cowered family and tenants alike.

He took, however, some of the good with the bad from his British source. He was never small. He never demeaned himself by denying the origins of his financial support. But while he did not hesitate to refer to his mother's late father as a "shameless rascal," he would insist at the same time, in the shrill, oddly masculine falsetto made fashionable in his circle by Theodore Roosevelt, that Cyrus Oates had been no worse than the grandsires of every other so-called gentleman in the room. And his snobbishness was always coupled with a sense of honor. A man who had shown courage in battle, especially one who had shared with him the charge up San Juan Hill behind the great Theodore, was his friend for life, no matter how short his family tree or how lean his purse.

But he could still be a terrible parent to live with. Mother, the only person, I think, he ever really loved, might have mitigated his occasional harshness to us, but she rarely made the effort. She seemed perfectly content with his tastes and pursuits, as if they were (perhaps truly) as much her own as his. She rode to hounds; she shot large and dangerous animals; and, blithely ignoring his contempt for golf, she played the game without him and scored under ninety.

The trouble with such parental unity was that it presented the young with a never questioned standard of values. Daddy's sneers had the deadly effect of annihilating other criteria. The things that Herman and Emily Vermeule didn't do, the clothes they didn't wear, the people they didn't see, the fanes they wouldn't worship in, the jokes that failed to amuse them, were made to seem ridiculous, if not downright vulgar. And try as I would, I found it hard not to be impressed by the sight of my parents at a hunt meet in the big field behind the Millbrook house, Daddy splendid in scarlet and white, Mother trim and neat in her black riding habit and tall silk hat, both mounted on magnificent bays and royally greeting the arrivals. They *did* make the rest of the world seem second class.

Of course, there were plenty of people who disagreed with Daddy and did not hesitate to tell him so. His two brothers were almost as opinionated as he, and when either of them dined with us we could expect a real shooting match. And my brothers, all three endowed with the Vermeule temperament, would sometimes quit the table and slam out of the house when Daddy became too outrageous. But I responded mostly by simply shrugging or shaking my head. Daddy rarely turned his big guns on women, and anyway, I knew I could never convince him.

But one night at a family dinner Daddy had to face a different sort of opponent, one who did not raise his voice. It was in the winter of 1920, and I was a junior at Barnard, where I had insisted on going — oh, yes, I *could* at times insist, despite my parents' opinion that higher education turned women into bluestockings. Our new guest was a twenty-nine-year-old lawyer, Ernest Stillman, who was the new partner in the downtown firm of Wentworth & Bailey, in charge of Daddy's legal affairs, hardly an enviable task. He was a large lean man with a square chin and a square, rather pasty face, an awkward manner and blue eyes of a surprising gentleness, which hardly meshed with his perfectly articulated and rather too frequent pronouncements of legal expertise. He was supposed to be the young "genius" of the firm, and I knew that Daddy was pleased to have him on his account, though he berated him in his absence as a "prig and a pompous ass." He never, however, complained to Mr. Wentworth about him, and I gathered that Mr. Stillman was a man who knew how to keep his clients (at least satisfied ones) in their place.

Daddy, who took a mild, critical interest in his children's social life and who knew I had been out the night before (he noticed more than one might have thought), tossed me a casual question in a conversational pause.

"How was your party, Alida?"

"Oh, all right, I guess. Just another dinner party."

"Who'd you sit next to?"

"Eddy Gould."

"No spawn of old Jay, I trust."

"A grandson, I believe."

"You didn't speak to him, I trust?"

"Oh, Daddy, don't be absurd. Why should he be blamed for what his grandfather did? Or didn't do?"

"He accepted his share of the loot, didn't he?"

"I really don't know what he accepted. And I don't care, either."

"Fine! So long as you don't trundle me home a son-in-law from that pigpen of parvenus."

I noted that Mr. Stillman, from across the table, was smiling at me with what I took to be sympathy. I appealed to him. "Would you believe, Mr. Stillman, to hear Daddy talk, that his own grandfather had been a robber baron?"

"And Cyrus Oates, if I am not mistaken, was associated with Jay Gould in securing control of the St. Louis Bridge Company in 1881." Here Mr. Stillman glanced at Daddy with an actual twinkle in his eye.

But Daddy may have been flattered by his lawyer's knowing so much about his family. "I admit, the Vermeules have had occasionally to replenish their depleted fortunes from unsavory wells. Old families have always done that. Nobody in England thought the less of Lord Rosebery for marrying a Rothschild."

"It's a pity, isn't it, that the Vermeules have no title," mused the intrepid Mr. Stillman. "It *does* help to cover over a misalliance. Perhaps you might revive the old one of patroon. Weren't your progenitors entitled to that?"

It was difficult to know whether this strange young man was riding Daddy or simply following his own scholastic bent. At any rate, he must have won some case arising out of the real estate in which our shrinking family fortunes were based, for Daddy took everything he said as a compliment.

"We were indeed patroons, Stillman. And might be still if

a handful of Virginia rebels hadn't taken it into their silly heads to deprive King George of his rightful heritage!"

After dinner Mr. Stillman sought me out in a corner of the parlor.

"I agreed with you about young Gould, Miss Vermeule. One shouldn't hold a man's grandfather against him."

"Particularly when one's own was such a crook."

He ventured a chuckle. "You're a bit hard on your father, Miss Vermeule. He sometimes talks for effect. That's his style. It's even part of his famous charm."

"I don't agree with you, Mr. Stillman. I think my father believes every word he utters. And I'm afraid I'm not always aware of the charm. Daddy squashes everything to death that doesn't fit in with his own credo."

"You're not afraid to talk back to him, though."

"But I never make a dent in him. How can a daughter do that? By going to college? I do, even though he sniffs. By working in settlement houses? I have. By reading all the books he tells me not to and going to every play he disapproves of? I have. And what does he do? Roars with laughter! Because he doesn't really care. Oh, I see that. But it makes it worse if you're a frump and a plain Jane and have a beautiful mother!"

"Oh, my dear Miss Vermeule, you're very far from being those things, believe me."

I blushed now, deeply mortified. I had been carried away by the indignation of my own introspection and forgotten that I was talking to a man.

"I'm sorry. I wasn't fishing for compliments."

"I wonder if you're not a good deal more emancipated from your father than you think. Which is perhaps why he asked me to sound you out on a matter of some delicacy. He may have feared that you might be short with him."

"What on earth are you talking about?"

"It concerns your aunt, Miss Isabel Vermeule. And her attorney of record, one Aaron Stern. Do you know the man?"

I hesitated. I did not quite like the way the question was put. "The man? Of course, I know him. Shouldn't I?"

"You say of course you know him, Miss Vermeule. But is it to be assumed that you should know your aunt's lawyer? I have many clients whose nieces wouldn't know me from the man in the moon."

Looking up and down the stiff young man, I thought this not unlikely. "But Mr. Stern is more than just Auntie's lawyer. He's her great friend. He's very apt to be there when I go out on a weekend."

"I see. And do you go out very often?"

"Oh, yes. Auntie and I are very close. Though I'm afraid I'm the only member of the family who is."

"Because your aunt is . . . so difficult?"

"She's not at all difficult, Mr. Stillman. She's just an individualist. Daddy's never appreciated her. Nor she him, I must admit. But what do you want to know about Mr. Stern? She's absolutely devoted to him, I can tell you that."

"Well, that, you see, is just what causes your father's apprehension."

"You mean because he thinks Mr. Stern may be after her money?"

It was Mr. Stillman's turn to hesitate. "Something like that."

"But how much money does Auntie have, anyway?" I exclaimed, exasperated by such a sordid suspicion. "She's always giving it away to her lame ducks. I'm sure Mr. Stern is much richer than she is. Isn't he supposed to be a brilliant lawyer?"

"And isn't there an old saying that nothing wants two million like one?"

"Is there? I wouldn't know." I was thoroughly indignant now. "Daddy probably thinks that's all a Jewish lawyer would care about. Well, we know what it is that *he* cares about! Mr. Stern is a wonderful man who's done more to make poor old Auntie happy than any member of the family. And I hope she leaves him every penny she has!"

Mr. Stillman's face was drawn with an alarm that I could not believe was entirely shammed. "Miss Vermeule, please do not think that I'm disagreeing with you! I was only doing what your father asked me to do."

I reined my temper. "Forgive me. But Daddy can be infuriating. I can put up with it at home, but he keeps reaching out into other parts of my life. I wish he'd leave Auntie alone. And now, if you'll excuse me, I must go upstairs and finish my reading for tomorrow's English class."

3   Aunt Isabel had become my refuge, my home away from home. Hers, anyway, was as different from mine as one could be. Let me describe her.

Physically, she was as tall and broad-shouldered as Daddy, and she resembled him facially, except that her features were heavier, her chin squarer, and her long straight white-blond hair, pulled back to a bun, gave her an air of pugnacity uncharming in a woman. Had she chosen to accent the masculine in her aspect, she might have fitted a part approved by her brothers as the "horsey Miss Vermeule," renowned for her firm seat in a cross-country hunt, for her loud free language and her tart warnings to those who rode on top of the hounds. But, perhaps too proud to compete with her younger brothers, she had elected instead the decidedly un-Vermeule role of priestess of the arts. In her lovely little Palladian villa in Westchester County she read and wrote (though never published) poetry, played the piano (with, I'm afraid, a rather heavy hand) and dedicated her beautiful garden to the cultivation of begonias, which she described as the "ultimate flower." She surrounded herself with a court of elderly virgins, occasional widows and young single men of greater artistic aspiration than accomplishment. One can imagine how my father and uncles described all of this. When I was present it was bad enough, but with ladies absent I have no doubt it was obscene.

Auntie's weakest point, and the one Daddy most seized upon to justify his branding her temple of the arts as "phony," was her drinking. Sometimes when I went out to Bedford, she would have taken to her bed and could not see me at all. At others she would sit on the porch without moving and drone on, her eyes half closed, about the heavenly beauty of Wagner's operas or Leonardo's oils. But most of the time she was to me a wonderful presence. With her I felt that my values were not all wrong, that there *was* a place in the world for shy, plain girls who liked to read and go to museums, that money and family and horses and mortifying dances and crude young men and silly gushing girls were not the only things in life. Oh, Auntie's bibulousness seemed to me a small price to pay — not that one really had to pay it — for all the wonderful things she had in *her* life. In every discussion that we had, and they were many and long, of the role of art even in the most mundane existences, she opened doors for me that always seemed to be slammed at home.

Sensing what she might be doing for me, she urged me to leave my parents and move in with her.

"Break away, dear child, break away. Before it's too late. It can be very catching, the Vermeule way of death. Because that's what it is, despite all of your father's stamping of his feet and gulping in fresh air."

"But Auntie, I'd have to commute into town every day for Barnard."

"Oh, pooh-pooh to Barnard. Aren't there thousands of books in this house?"

And so there were, of every sort, in every imaginable binding, all along the corridors, even in the cellar. "But what about my degree?"

"Who needs a degree?"

"*I* may, if I have to support myself. The way Daddy spends money, heaven knows what any of us will be left. I don't want to have to marry a rich old man who needs a nurse."

"Heavens above, I should hope not! Why not a rich young man who wants a love of a wife?"

"Well, I won't say I'm hopeless, but I still want to be able to look after myself."

"You know you can always depend on me, dearie."

"But, Auntie, I don't want to depend on anybody!"

Sometimes she would go too far in her abuse of my parents — she had her moments of being just as violent as Daddy — and my loyalty would reemerge.

"Daddy and Mother are not total philistines, you know. They read some good books. They go to art galleries. Daddy even collects Mucha posters."

"They dip, my love, they dip. They stick a cautious toe in the cold waters of beauty and waggle it. You have to *give* yourself to art. Hold nothing back."

And indeed when she played a record of Gadski and Jean de Reszke in *Tristan*, she appeared to go into a sort of trance.

Of course, I could see that this was extreme. How, as my father's daughter, could I not? But there was still something in it that strongly appealed to me. When Auntie and I read passages aloud from *The Ring and the Book* (she was a great Browning fan), I would be transported, not to Rome in the late seventeenth century, but to the poet's concept of it, and in imagining what it must have been like for him to have put this together, I fancied that I entered a bit into the joy of creation. But could one make a life out of simple response to another's act?

Auntie's affirmative answer to this question was eloquent. "Of course you can! A perfect response is a perfect life. What is art without it but a song warbled in the desert? Isn't that true of religion? Mystics and monks don't need to *do* anything. Once the light has entered their souls, their lives are complete. Henry James Senior believed that when an idea was perfectly conceived in the mind, it was almost a pity, certainly a diminishment, to execute it in paint or in print. Ah, there it is, Alida! A great poet like Emily Dickinson had no need to publish. She hardly needed to write. The poem within herself was the supreme reality."

"But if her friends hadn't printed her poems, we wouldn't have them!"

"Don't worry, my dear. The friends always will."

"Trust them to!" came from the doorway, the voice of a man who had evidently overheard our colloquy. "And I, my dear Isabel, have brought you a vulgar bit of print which, when adorned with your signature, will enable your humble servant to dispose of that pesky Market Street property for a sum you may dedicate to the muses. If you and your clever niece will descend a moment from Parnassus and stop your sensitive nostrils, we may spend a few minutes manuring the lowly fields of commerce."

It was thus that Aaron Stern would break in upon us. He would have been a most impressive man had he been taller and straighter. As it was, his diminutive stature was almost compensated for by his beautiful pale eagle-like face, his dark laughing eyes and his thick, lustrous, black curly hair which descended on his high forehead in a triangle. I can see in retrospect why he struck my family as sinister, a grinning demon slipping into Auntie's never-never land of Palladian innocence. But to me he was always a delightful being, whose impudence and occasional crudeness gave zest to his infectious good humor and whose encyclopedic knowledge of art and literature was quite as impressive as his expertise in the smallest print of the law. I fully sympathized with what the Vermeules called "Isabel's infatuation."

Auntie responded enthusiastically even to Mr. Stern's vulgar jokes. At one of these she would clap a hand over her mouth, as if she were trying to keep something in, open her eyes wide and then suddenly erupt in a peal of violent laughter. I had learned some facts of life from my friends at Barnard, including the fact of lesbianism, and it would not have surprised me if a woman as aggressively single and as stalwartly built as Auntie should have entertained inclinations, however much repressed, for her own sex, but there was no mistaking her kittenish attitudes towards Mr. Stern for anything but flirtation. Perhaps, having steeled herself from youth against the upper-class sportsmen exemplified by her brothers, she may have left unguarded the fragile little girl within herself who might now see ultra-masculine qualities in a type of man whom the outer woman had been raised to regard as "common" and overfamiliar.

Mr. Stern applauded my going to college and had even once suggested that I should go on to law school. This last was elicited by my correct answer to a question that he jokingly tossed to me about a mortgage during a business discussion he was having with Auntie.

"Now there's a young woman who's not going to spend her life dropping cards and pouring tea! Where did you learn about liens, Alida?"

"I'm taking a course in history of law at Barnard. It's very general, though."

"It's still a start." He turned to Auntie. "And when this bright niece of yours becomes an attorney, Isabel, goodbye to old Aaron! She'll send me packing."

"I don't keep you just for law, my friend," Auntie replied, with a snort that was meant to imply, no doubt, her Olympian scorn for all forms of jurisprudence. "And I want no lawyers from my own family, thank you very much. Even you, Alida dearest. I can just see your dad looking over your shoulder as you drafted my will to be sure I had left all my lovely things to the Vermeules." Here she paused to gaze dreamily up at a large Alma-Tadema painting of two Roman damsels in a marble tower looking down on a trireme floating on an azure sea. "I can even hear him dictating to you: 'All the rest, residue and remainder' — is that the phrase, Aaron? — 'to my brothers and their issue then living in' . . . how do you say it?"

" 'In equal shares per stirpes'!" Mr. Stern responded exuberantly. "But your aunt has other plans, Alida. Can we tell her, Isabel? I know we used to suggest that she take a walk in the garden when we discussed your will, but I think we can trust her now, don't you?" When Auntie nodded, he continued in a confidential tone: "Your aunt doesn't feel bound by the old Knickerbocker code that money must follow the blood. That every dollar has a ticket on it, as a Vermeule buck, or a Livingston buck, or what have you."

"Most of ours are lowly Oates bucks."

Stern slapped his knee. "I love this girl, Isabel! All the more reason to put those lowly bucks to a better use. Your aunt, Alida, has conceived the noble scheme of creating a foundation to run this beautiful little palazzo as a haven for working artists and writers. What do you think of that?"

"I think it's a wonderful idea!"

Auntie was always talking about her imminent demise, but like many who do so, she didn't really believe in it. I had been told, however, by her doctor that it was only too probable, that her weak heart could not much longer bear her weight, particularly in view of her heavy drinking. I was thus prepared for the grim news, not long after this will discussion, that she had suffered a grave coronary. I wanted to go to Bedford and help with the nursing, but she did not wish to be seen in her bedridden state and sent me word that she loved me but had "turned her face to the wall."

"It appears that she'll see no one but a man from that Aaron Stern's firm," Daddy growled at me one morning at breakfast. "What the devil do you suppose *he's* up to?"

"A man from the firm? You mean, Mr. Stern himself?"

"No, the housekeeper tells me it's one of his partners."

I supposed this would be some expert on the law of establishing foundations, and I couldn't help smiling to myself at the prospect of the cries of outrage with which the assembled Vermeules would greet the reading of Auntie's new will.

But what I never dreamed of was that *I* would be equally appalled. Auntie's second and fatal heart attack followed the first by only a month, and the morning after the funeral Mother came to my room as I was getting ready to go to college, and closed the door quietly behind her.

"I'm afraid I must ask you to be a little late this morning, dear. I have something important to talk to you about."

When Mother spoke in this tone, even my brothers

obeyed. Serene, pale, but strong and straight of figure, with the loveliest blue-grey eyes and silver-tinted wavy hair, regally handsome even in the short dresses of the twenties, she could be a figure of quiet authority on the rare occasions when she chose to be, even to Daddy.

"I told your father that *I* would talk to you. He gets too excited. This is what has happened. Aunt Isabel has left her whole estate to that lawyer."

"To Mr. Stern? But I knew that."

"You *knew* it?"

"Yes, but it's not for him. He's to run her place as a sort of workshop for writers and artists."

Mother looked at me gravely. "Aunt Isabel told you that?"

"Yes! At least I think she did. Or maybe Mr. Stern did."

"Maybe Mr. Stern did indeed. Your father wants you to know that you will be called as a witness in the suit he and your uncles will bring to break the will."

"Break the will?" I was shaking with instant indignation. "Buy why? Couldn't Auntie do what she wanted with her own money?"

"Yes. *If* that was what she wanted. But was it? The will says nothing about a home for artists. Everything is left outright to Mr. Stern. Without a word of instruction or condition. *Outright*, Alida."

My mind tumbled about. "Well, maybe Auntie trusted him to set up her foundation. Maybe there wasn't time to work out all the legal details in the will. Maybe they just had to seize the shortest way."

"That's what they seem to have done. The very shortest."

"Anyway, is it worth a nasty lawsuit? How much money did Auntie leave?"

"Very little. She'd been spending capital for years. But that was not, it seems, what Mr. Stern was after."

"It was the house! Of course, I told you so!"

"It was *not* the house, dear. It was the land behind the house. That whole beautiful valley of the best real estate in Bedford. Seven hundred acres of it, which Isabel bought for a song more than forty years ago. Daddy thinks it's worth well over a million. And it just so happens, as a neighbor of Isabel's has already informed us, that Mr. Stern owns an adjacent plot of two hundred acres. He obviously plans a development that will make him the landlord of Bedford."

I flung my briefcase on the bed. There would be no college for me that day.

"I can hardly believe anything so horrible!"

Mother came over to fold me in her arms in one of her rare embraces, all the more wonderful for that very quality.

"Ah, my dear girl, I'm so sorry. And you loved your aunt so much. I hope it will give you some consolation to know that you were the best niece in the world."

4 When I went down to Ernest Stillman's office to go over my testimony for the approaching trial, Daddy insisted on coming with me. We found our young lawyer as cool and self-possessed as he had been at our family dinner, but I could not now resent his questions about Auntie, and I was amused by the deft way he handled Daddy.

"It's an outrage that we even have to take this shyster to court!" the latter fulminated. "There ought to be some kind of summary disbarment for an attorney who drafts a will leaving his client's property to himself."

"But he didn't draft the will himself, Mr. Vermeule. He is evidently familiar with the Canons of Legal Ethics. He took the precaution of having one of his partners perform that office, and he absented himself, according to his answer filed in court, from all testamentary conferences as well as from the actual execution of the document."

"And you *believe* all that?"

"I do, sir. Mr. Stern would have been a fool to have done otherwise. And whatever you think of him, you cannot call him *raca*, to use a biblical term."

Stillman now proceeded to question me about the critical weekend, only six weeks before Auntie's death, that I had spent with her in Bedford. I told him how Mr. Stern had motored out from the city on Sunday to lunch, how he and Auntie had seemed on the best of terms, how his conversation had been lively and amusing, and how he had provided an agreeable diversion on a dreary rainy day. Daddy became restive.

"Let's get down to brass tacks, Alie. The guy fawned on her disgustingly, didn't he? Wasn't he oily and insinuating? Ugh! I can just see him bowing and scraping."

"Please, Mr. Vermeule, allow me to conduct the inquiry. I think it will be more expeditious that way. But so long as you have brought up the topic of Mr. Stern's outward demonstrations, let me put this question to your daughter." Ernest turned back to me. "Could you describe to me how Mr. Stern greeted and took leave of your aunt? Did he simply shake her hand or did he offer her some form of embrace?"

"He kissed her, didn't he, Alie? And right on the lips, too, isn't it so? A big juicy smack, I'll bet."

"Mr. Vermeule, I must protest. You are leading the witness."

"We're not in court, man! I can remind my own daughter

of what she told me herself, can't I? Didn't you tell me he kissed her, Alie?"

"But not on the lips, Daddy. At least I don't think so."

"You don't *think* so! Or did you look away in disgust? I couldn't blame you. For a man like that to touch my sister's hand with the tip of his fingers would be to defile her."

Without responding to this, Ernest put another question to me.

"May I infer, Miss Vermeule, that such osculation as there might have been was what is called cheek to cheek?"

"That would have been more like it, yes."

"And is not such a form of greeting considered, even in high social circles, an innocent expression of friendship between a lady and a gentleman? You may recall —"

"*Gentleman!* I like that!"

"Please, Mr. Vermeule, let me finish. You may recall, Miss Vermeule, if you are, like myself, a devotee of the bard, how Roderigo, in *Othello*, answers Iago's insinuation that Desdemona has been 'paddling' with Cassio's hand."

"I'm afraid I'm not that much of a Shakespeare scholar, Mr. Stillman."

"Allow me to refresh your memory. He says that he *had* observed it, but that it was only courtesy. Was that how you interpreted Mr. Stern's gesture to your aunt?"

"Lechery!" Daddy shouted. "It's right there in the play, if I recall it correctly."

"But now you are quoting Iago, sir."

"And isn't Iago's strong language what we need to describe Stern's filthy conduct? You should have learned by now, my boy, that in dealing with skunks you have to give out a stench yourself. Jew shysters of Stern's type do so much screaming and shouting in a courtroom that the pale cast of truth doesn't always get over to a jury. You have to adapt your own words to their inflated vocabulary."

"I'm afraid that is hardly consistent with the ethics of our profession."

"But you have to start with certain basic facts and work back from there," Daddy insisted hotly. "And the first of these is that a woman brought up like my sister could not possibly have disinherited her own family for a beast like Stern unless she was off her rocker. Can you suggest even *one* other reason for her doing so?"

"I think I can. She might have felt detached from relatives who, however devoted, were essentially occupied with their own lives. She may have felt that Stern was more than just her lawyer. That he was a true friend who found her congenial and companionable. She may even have believed that she offered him something that nobody else had, that she —"

"A silly old-maid notion that he was only too quick to nurture!"

I had been much struck by Ernest's reasoning. I had not believed that any lawyer hired by my father and his brothers could have been so concerned with truth. "Oh, *do* listen to him, Daddy!"

Daddy now glared from me to Ernest. "Well, if you two think my sister was in her right mind when she gave her share of the family money — money she had no moral right to alienate from her own brothers — to that bloodsucker, I suggest that Stillman is not the man for this case!"

I gazed with dismay at Ernest. Would he rise and with a formal bow open the door to indicate that the interview was at an end? But he did no such thing. He nodded slowly, as if taking in the client's proposition.

"I am not assuming, Mr. Vermeule, that our defendant is guiltless of exercising undue influence in the making of your sister's will. On the contrary, it seems to me not improbable that we may be able to establish that he did just that. But I never go into court until I have explored every interpretation of the given facts. If I don't do that, I deserve to be faced with opposing counsel who *have*."

Daddy, after a heavy silence, nodded reluctantly. "Very well. Do it your way. After all, you're the doctor."

"And may I request a favor of you? May I continue this examination of your daughter alone?"

I was afraid for a minute that he had gone too far, but Daddy simply scowled and left the room.

In the discussion that now ensued Ernest never once suggested that I alter my testimony in any way to favor the side of the plaintiffs. He seemed interested solely in putting the true facts before a jury and allowing them to decide. He warned me, however, that I should not, any more than my father, prejudge the case, that the question of undue influence between a clever lawyer and an impressionable lonely lady client was a delicate one.

I was impressed by his argument and greatly relieved at being rid of the responsibility of having to decide for myself which was right between my impassioned relatives and the "clever lawyer."

It was partly this and partly my surprised amusement at the courtly way he escorted me to the reception hall that caused me to accept his parting invitation that I should dine with him at Sherry's the following Saturday night.

"Do we discuss the case even on weekends?" I tried to keep the question from sounding arch.

"Everything *but* the case, I hope," he responded with a bow. "I shall endeavor not to bore my charming guest with business matters."

Actually, we dined together not only that Saturday night but the two following. I wasn't quite sure why, but it didn't seem to commit me to anything. He was certainly not ro-

mantic in manner. He didn't offer me extravagant compliments, nor did he do anything as crude as to try to kiss me
in the taxicab. If he was a "beau," I had never had one like
him. He talked all the time, much too much; he seemed to
know everything in the world: literature, astronomy, geol-
ogy, even zoology. But oddly enough, he didn't appear to be
showing off. It was as if he wanted to share his lore with
me, or as if he were somehow trying to pick his way through
it *to* me, as if I could catch in the gentle appeal of his eyes,
over the wall of his excess learning, a whisper of: "Help me,
help me to get out!"

How would another girl have reacted to a monologue like
this one?

"Anatole France amuses us in his tale "Le Procurateur de
Judée" when he depicts the aging Pontius Pilate, discussing
old times with another survivor, as unable to recall the crucifixion. *'Jésus?'* he repeats, rubbing his brow. *'Jésus de Naza-
reth? Je ne me rappelle pas.'* Of course, France picked up the
idea from Renan's *Vie de Jésus*. But from what scholars since
have gleaned, the trial of Christ may have made more of a
public impression than France's story would imply, and it
seems at least questionable if his name would have struck no
chord in the venerable Roman's memory. Incidentally, I was
much excited by the recent excavation in Caesarea of the
base of a pillar bearing Pilate's name and the date of a year
in his administration. Do you realize that it is the only contemporary archaeological, epigraphic or numismatic evidence that he ever lived?"

No, I didn't. And cared less. But Ernest was always perfectly willing to be interrupted, even to have the topic
abruptly switched. He was delighted to answer my most
banal questions about his profession. Should a lawyer rep-
resent a defendant he knows to be guilty? If a client tells a
lie on cross-examination, should he expose him to the court?

Should he draw a will for a testator which unjustly disinherits a child? Ernest would eagerly explain the subtleties of ethical conduct, seeking to persuade me that litigation as practiced by the good members of his beloved profession was the only practical way of establishing disputed truth.

He bored me, yet I liked him. And I could not help but be flattered by the attention of so remarkable a man. How he felt about me I certainly could not tell by anything he said or even looked, but I felt sure he could never be anything but serious in any position he took. If it should come to a proposal . . . well, that would be absurd. I felt no love for him, only sympathy verging on something not too far from pity. He was so odd! But I didn't have to worry about complications yet. He was surely a man who would need plenty of time.

5

On the first day of the trial I was much impressed by Ernest's forensic abilities. He became a different man in court. Gone now were the arid scholastic jokes and the pedagogical mannerisms. The new Ernest was succinct, impeccably polite to witnesses of both sides, deferential to jurors, clear and cogent in his questions and comments. He put me on the stand, but only briefly, to establish Stern's proposed plan for the artists' haven; I was not cross-examined. Daddy, when I resumed my seat beside him, was visibly restless.

"Why is he handling these crooks with kid gloves?" he whispered to me crossly. "When do the fireworks begin? Or do they?"

They began, alas, the next day. Fireworks, however, was

not the word; icebergs would have been more appropriate. Ernest waxed colder and drier as he examined the witnesses for the plaintiffs: Auntie's two maids and various members of her little "court," all of whom obviously detested Stern. He chillingly explored every vulgar detail of the defendant's conduct with Auntie: every off-color joke, every liberty taken, every kiss and bear hug. He would turn silently to the jury as he made each point, his eyebrows slightly raised, as if to put a mute rhetorical question as to whether they had ever imagined such deportment between attorney and client. He built his case like a skilled architect. Upon the laid foundation of Stern's intimate and insinuating approach to his elderly client he erected the structure of the lawyer's fraudulent plan for an artists' colony, adding the picture of a naïve and dazzled old maid, listening with eager ears and shining eyes, and, finally, he hit the jury with the bare fact of the total absence of any such gift in the testament. He then established that Stern had sent cases of liquor to Auntie on her birthday and Christmas, with what sinister intent to disintegrate further her already addled brain the jury might deduce for themselves. But his great coup was in producing a letter from the defendant, a widower, to his client actually proposing marriage!

I was outraged. The letter, at least to me, was obviously just another of Stern's crude jokes, designed to titillate my poor aunt, but with no insidious intent. It seemed to me that Ernest had now joined forces with my family to achieve a brutal revocation of Auntie's gift to the legatee of her choice. They were proclaiming the principle that if a silly old woman attempted to leave money away from her next of kin, any tactic was justified to circumvent her.

Two things now happened at once. Daddy gave vent to a loud, jeering laugh, causing a just reproof from the bench.

And I saw Aaron Stern jump up from his counsel's bench and rush from the courtroom. Obeying a sudden impulse, I hurried after him and caught up with him in the corridor.

"Oh, please, Mr. Stern, may I talk to you?"

For a second his exasperated countenance showed no recognition. Then he responded. "Haven't I had to take enough from your horrible family?"

"But you don't understand! I'm on your side. I know you wanted to use the place for Auntie's artists."

His look was searching. "Do you? Well, you're right. And suppose I'd developed the land as well? Wouldn't that have meant more dough to support the project?"

"Of course it would! And Auntie would have wanted you to be compensated. After all, it would have been a big job."

The searching look now became suspicious, but, probably deducing that I was not sarcastic, he then shrugged. "Anyway, you can tell your old man that I'm ready to throw in the sponge. I'll settle the case for a hundred g's."

"But why? They haven't *proved* anything."

"No, and they won't. But your aunt's estate isn't big enough for what this is doing to my reputation. God, it's murder! The Vermeules have nothing to learn from the Jews about crucifixion!"

"I'm ashamed of the lot of them! *And* of their lawyer!"

"Oh, that Stillman's all right. He's a smart one. I'd take him in my firm any day."

Saying which, he hurried off.

I didn't go back to the courtroom; I went home instead. That night, when I told Daddy about Stern's proposed settlement, he uttered a whoop of triumph and hurried to the telephone to inform his counsel. Ernest had just heard of the offer himself from Stern's lawyer; it was agreed at once between them that it should be accepted.

When Ernest called the following afternoon to get Daddy to sign the settlement papers, I remained in my room on the pretext of homework, but when he was leaving and sent word upstairs to ask if he could see me for just a minute, I could hardly refuse. I found him standing in the front hall with a big bunch of lilies in his hand. But when he offered them to me, I stepped abruptly back.

"What are those for?" I demanded. "To make me forget?"

"Forget what?"

"All the mean little ways you achieved your victory."

Indignation now topped his astonishment. "What was mean about them? Everyone thought I did very well! Even your rarely uncritical sire."

"But Daddy would have done anything to beat poor Mr. Stern. He didn't believe he deserved fair play."

"*Poor* Mr. Stern! I thought even you, Alida, had agreed he was pretty bad."

"Oh, bad." I shrugged angrily. "So bad you had to crucify him? So bad you had to falsify all his silly vulgar jokes? So bad you had to turn him into the mustachioed villain of a melodrama? Shame on you, Mr. Stillman!"

"You don't believe he used undue influence on your aunt?"

"I suppose he used what influence he could. And I daresay he wouldn't have cared if it was undue. I think he felt as much entitled to her estate as any of her family. And *wasn't* he? Can you even compare what he and Daddy contributed to her happiness? The real point isn't whether he tried to use undue influence, but whether he succeeded. I'm not at all sure that Auntie wouldn't have left him the estate even if she'd had a completely independent lawyer. Of her own free mind and will!"

"But I was only doing my job, Alida! Isn't that what every lawyer worth his salt would have done?"

"And what's his salt worth?"

"Is there a better way?"

" 'I am the way, the truth and the life'!" This was going pretty far, but I knew that Ernest was a devout High Episcopalian, and I was very worked up.

"But we have to be practical, don't we?"

"I don't know if we have to be, but we certainly are."

Poor Ernest at this seemed to wilt. He placed the flowers on the hall table and turned to the door. But then he faced me again, bitter as I had never seen him.

"I suppose this is my dismissal. But do you know something? This afternoon, just before leaving the office, Mr. Wentworth called me in. He did not feel about my little victory as you do. He said he'd been waiting for the end of the case, which he was sure I would win, to give me the good news of a raise in my percentage. I at last felt in a position where I could offer a Mrs. Stillman all the comforts that a Miss Vermeule enjoys. I was going to ask you to be my wife."

I had never imagined such a conflict of emotions as now overcame me. As I peered at that woebegone face in the darkening hall, it occurred to me that I had been an ass to make such an issue about a lawyer's doing what any other, even the most honest, would have done, and yet it irritated me that he should somehow have put me in the wrong. I certainly didn't want to marry him, but I also didn't want it to end like this, here and now, leaving me with the memory of those hauntingly reproachful eyes. Damn you, Ernest Stillman, I cried to myself, what are you trying to do to me?

"Very well, I'm sorry. Perhaps I've been too hasty about the whole thing. I don't really know why I should give a hoot *who* gets Aunt Isabel's money. Maybe we'd better not see each other for a while. It all seems to have been rather too much for both of us."

He looked very white at this and left the house without another word. I was afraid he had taken it as a sarcastic and final dismissal. I was about to go to the top of the stoop and call after him, but then I reflected: Why? Wasn't it better this way?

🌿 🌿 🌿

6 🌿 🌿 🌿 The next three months were discontented ones for me. Ernest made no sign, and I supposed that he regarded our rupture as final. When Mother asked me if I should like her to invite him to dinner at the house, I said no and then told her briefly of his aborted proposal. She made no comment, but looked pensive, and I knew she had told Daddy when he brought the subject up, in his own awkward fashion, when he and I were breakfasting alone one morning.

"If you don't mind my saying so, Alie, you haven't lost exactly a pearl in Stillman."

"I *do* mind your saying so."

"But the guy has ink in his veins, not blood!"

"I'd really rather not talk about it, Daddy."

"I know he's a brilliant lawyer and all that, but let me ask you just one thing. Has he ever had a girlfriend before you? I mean a *real* girlfriend."

"You mean a mistress? I wouldn't know."

"No, no, I didn't mean a mistress. Though that's not altogether beside the point. How old is he, anyway? Thirty plus? What I'm getting at is, does the guy have any notion of how to handle women?"

"Do you think I need so much handling?"

"Yes, damn it all! Any worthwhile woman does. And you can be a spitfire, my dear; make no mistake about *that*. The question is, can a legal Galahad, pure as driven snow, handle a spitfire?"

At this I simply left the table. I knew that Daddy was trying to be kind, but I could barely control my bitterness over his dragging the standards of the Vermeules into my private life to make a buffoon of the one man who had wanted to marry me. And the horrible thing, as always, was how effective his mocking was!

I don't know what would have happened to my life had Mother not at last decided to intervene. She had a way of doing this to her children on rare occasions, after she had silently, and at some length, pondered over their problems. When did she do it? Riding back from the hunt? On the golf course? At a dull dinner party? Perhaps at all these times.

In town she had tea every day at five, and if she was alone I would sometimes quit my college homework and come down to join her. On one such afternoon she made me a surprising proposition.

"Now that you no longer have Aunt Isabel to confide in, how about giving your ma a try?"

"But you and Daddy always thought Auntie was such a *silly*. Why would you want to take a silly's place?"

"She may have had her silly side, but I still think she was good for you."

"How? As a grim warning of what can happen to an unmarried maiden?"

Mother's silence, as she now poured a cup, seemed to mark a period needed to let my irritability fade away. Her long pale blue tea gown, so much better adapted to her fine figure than the styles of the day, gave her the air of a priestess in an opera. Norma, I vaguely recalled.

"I do not think, my dear, that you should bracket me with your father. While it is true that I thought Isabel oversentimental about art and pretty things, I certainly did not regard her as irrational, as your father did. I knew she was giving you something that you weren't getting at home, and I counted on your good sense to separate the wheat from the chaff."

For a moment I feared I was going to burst into tears. I wanted her consolation so desperately, and yet I was miserably subject to an ugly urge to kick it away. "Oh, Mother, I'd love to confide in you, but you've never cared about any of the things I've cared about! You've always favored the boys in everything they do. When Tom won that squash championship at the Racquet Club last year, you went on and on about it. You know he's your pet."

"I don't know any such thing. I suppose it's not possible for a mother to love all her children equally all the time, and of course I know that no child will accept second best. It has to be all or nothing. But they make a mistake. Even my second best, *if* that's what it is, might be better than nothing."

I was humbled, but still resistant. "But how could you really help me? Your life has always been so . . . so perfect. You *do* things so well. And I'm such a mess."

"Let me tell you something about my 'perfect' life. It wasn't always as it is. My mother, as you know, was a divorced woman in a world that still didn't accept divorce. But she made them accept *her*. She may not have had big money, or beauty, or even very much charm, but she had a terrible will power. She carved out her own place in society, but she couldn't do quite the same for me. I splashed along in her wake, but I was always a bit of a waif. Until your father came along. He used to say that his bride would have to have looks *or* money, because the last woman to have both was Consuelo Vanderbilt. Anyway, I qualified, and it certainly wasn't for my money." Here Mother smiled, even, I thought, rather complacently. "And after we were married, I found, all of a sudden, that I *fitted* in. Fitted in perfectly to his sports-loving world. And what is more, I *loved* fitting in. I guess you have to have lived on the rim to know the joy of that. And do you know something? It *lasts!* The joy, I mean. At least it did with me. Does that sound terribly stuffy and unadventurous and dull?"

"No," I lied, for I wanted her to go on.

"I'm the squarest little peg in the squarest little hole! And that's what you have to find, my dear. A hole you fit into. Of course, it doesn't have to be one like mine. That would never suit you, I know. You can find a much bigger and more interesting one. But you won't find it until you give up being so angry at people."

"Angry at whom?"

"Angry at your father for being what you call a philistine. For his feeling that he is morally as well as legally entitled to your aunt's estate. And angry at Ernest Stillman for winning Daddy's case in the only way he could. And I believe you are even angry with Mr. Stern for trying to grab all of Isabel's property, even if he *did* mean to carve out a small piece for her artists. But they are all violent men, my dear, each firmly believing he's utterly justified in what he's doing. You're never going to get any of them to change their opinion. And does it really matter? Save your energy for things that do."

"And what are they?"

"Ah, that's for you to decide."

"But how shall I start?"

"*I'd* start by making things up with Mr. Stillman."

"Mother, do you think I should *marry* Ernest Stillman?"

"Did I say that? At any rate, a girl could do worse."

"Even if Daddy thinks he's an ass?"

"I thought we'd agreed he was a genius."

"A genius can be an ass. I daresay many geniuses are. Outside of the field of their genius."

"And so you now adopt Daddy's standards?"

"No, no, of course not!"

"But yes, yes, dear Alida, if you allow them to anger you. That's just my point again. Anger will get you nowhere. I don't suggest you marry Mr. Stillman. But I do suggest that you go and see the poor man."

"Why is he a poor man? Because I won't have him?"

"That might be one reason. Mr. Wentworth tells me he's having some sort of breakdown. A depression, I think it's called. Apparently he has them periodically."

"And where is he?" I asked in alarm. "In a sanitorium?"

"No, it's evidently not that bad. He's taking a month's leave of absence from the firm and is staying with his old mother in Salisbury. Right near us in Millbrook. Why don't you go and see him next weekend?"

7

The house was attractive, a small, square, two-story structure of grey stone with freshly painted green shutters on the windows. Ernest's widowed mother met me at the door; she was very tall and skinny with a dark wrinkled face and a warm, broad smile. She struck me at once as a lady with the confidence of a strong and benevolent character.

"Come in, my dear, come in. Ernest is out walking, but he should be back any minute now. Let me give you a cup of coffee."

She led me through a dark interior where I had a passing glimpse of old books, surely loved, on long shelves and what might have been Old Master drawings on the walls, to a small immaculate kitchen where we drank our coffee at a table that was probably used for meals when there were no guests.

Mrs. Stillman treated me as an old friend of her son's, without even a hint of romantic complications. She was frank about his ailment.

"His doctor says he works too hard, and that may be a part of it. But I have a notion that these things are largely inherited. His father had periods of depression, though he always came out of them. I never let them worry me too much. I tell Ernest: 'Come up to your old ma and breathe a little country air,' and that usually turns him around. And do you know something else? Ernest is never nicer than when he's down. He and I have had some of our dearest times together just when you'd least think so."

I saw what she meant as soon as Ernest came in, looking much less stiff than usual in grey flannels and an open shirt. He made no undue fuss over me, accepting my visit as the natural friendly act of a neighbor. There was no reference to the case, nor did his mother make any move to leave us alone. We three chatted about the birds he had seen on his walk, and the hunt in Millbrook, and why my parents loved it so, and wasn't it hard on the foxes, and what a poor president Harding was, and had Mrs. Woodrow Wilson taken too much power into her own hands after her husband's stroke. None of us cared unduly about any of the topics, yet the conversation was somehow disproportionately pleasant. Ernest seemed to have lost his pomposity; his language was much simpler, and his quiet smile had charm. I felt, not anything so crude as that I'd been forgiven for my harshness to him after the trial, but that the episode belonged to another world.

When I left, Mrs. Stillman took advantage of my going upstairs to the bathroom to have two words with me alone.

"If you could find a moment to drop in on us again, it would be a great thing for Ernest. I could just *feel* the clouds lifting today."

I had an important week of classes at Barnard ahead, for graduation was only a month away, but I knew, with a light skip of my heart, that I was going to cut them.

Daddy and Mother said nothing when I told them that I would stay up in the house alone for a few days and not return with them to town. I said it would be a good occasion to study. Of course, they didn't believe me, but then they both considered Barnard a complete waste of time.

Ernest and I took long walks in the early spring countryside during the next three days. We talked of everything but our own relationship; the easy and relaxed atmosphere of the first morning persisted. I was happy, and chatted about myself and my problems with an ease I had not known before. But when I came to the subject of my father, he took a much milder view than mine.

"Daddy's antediluvian!" I protested. "He really believes that men were born just to be warriors and women just to bear children. He went almost wild when Wilson wouldn't let him and Colonel Roosevelt go abroad to get killed in the trenches. As if General Pershing didn't have something better to do than worry about two crazy old men!"

"Yes, your father truly believed that the country needed some bloodletting," Ernest mused. "He thinks men degenerate in too long a peace. And he felt genuinely sorry for me because a fibrillating heart kept me out of the service. I know some people think that such belligerence may mask a fear of cowardice. But that's certainly not true of him. He is quite fearless, I'm sure. What he doesn't realize is that war cannot

give courage to those who already have it or supply it to
those who don't. It doesn't make men; it simply kills them."

I felt as he said this that he might recognize fearlessness in
Daddy because of the same quality in himself. That morning
in the kitchen his mother had asked him to get rid of a huge
spider on the wall. The calm way in which he had caught
the ugly creature in his bare hands and put it out of doors
rather than kill it had, for me anyway, a Saint Francis air.
That may sound silly, and I know that most men do not
share my horror of large insects, but I had still the odd
conviction that he would have faced even a dangerous beast
with the same coolness.

"The great thing about both your parents, Alida, is that
they find happiness in what they're doing. And, after all,
they don't hurt anyone. Even the foxes usually get away.
Sometimes I think there is so little real happiness on the
globe that to get even a small slice of it may be a valid
purpose in life. For so many people it is arbitrarily snatched
away."

This was as near as he came to mentioning his own depressed state, and I was deeply moved. It was then that the
idea first took hold of me that I might really help him to
blow away these clouds of melancholy.

I do not know, even today, just how Ernest managed to
express his love for me. He did not say a word about it, or
even take my hand as we walked. But from his gentle manner, his kind and humorous inquiries into every aspect of
my college and home life, his concern that I should be cutting classes, there emanated for me the sense of a powerful
emotion that gripped me as strongly as if I had been hugged
by unreleasing arms. When I thought of Daddy's crude concept of what a man should be, I could laugh almost pity-
ingly.

When Ernest repeated his proposal of some months past, he did it, not surprisingly for him, with a quotation from a classic. Returning from our walk, we had paused at the gate of his mother's little rose garden.

"Do you remember what Darcy said to Elizabeth at the end of *Pride and Prejudice*? 'You are too generous to trifle with me. If your feelings are still what they were last April, tell me so at once. *My* affections and wishes are unchanged.'"

I smiled. "Except it wasn't last April."

"I but follow the text. With the hope of the same happy ending."

And so we became engaged.

Ernest's depression lifted with our new happiness, and he returned to his work at Wentworth & Bailey. We agreed to be married a month after my graduation from Barnard. My parents offered me congratulations so hearty that I could easily see they had not been optimistic about my matrimonial prospects. But I no longer cared.

There was only one thing that bothered me. With the return of his mental health there also returned some of Ernest's old manner. One night, at a dinner party given us by one of his partners, the conversation fell upon the relative advantages of a republic and a constitutional monarchy. Ernest startled the table by maintaining that the British crown was an elective one. But then, alas, he went on.

"It has been one, actually, since the Act of Succession. Not only did Parliament establish Mary II as queen regnant over the undoubted rights of her father and half-brother; it placed her consort, William III, as co-monarch with right of succession, even though he had no dynastic claim to the throne. It is true that he was a grandson of Charles I, but on the distaff side. And then Parliament went even further. It raised William over Anne, Mary's own sister. And on

Anne's demise without issue, the good Lords and Commons passed over dozens of Catholic princes with better claims to clap the crown on the fat German Protestant head of George I. If that is not an election, pray show me one."

I suffered atrociously during this lecture. All the household gods of the Vermeules seemed to be laughing at me from the mantel on which they had suddenly appeared. If I should marry this man, would I have to persuade him to give up social life? Or to convince him to go out without me? I recalled Auntie telling me of a friend of hers who had consulted an associate of the great Doctor Freud in Vienna. Her "free association" had been fatally blocked because she could not bring herself to tell him he had bad breath. Some people, perhaps, prefer death to candor.

Ernest showed his surprise across the room after dinner when he saw me drink two stiff whiskeys. In the taxi taking me home, he inquired gently if something had occurred to upset me.

"Yes!" I exclaimed. "You were a bore! You were a terrible bore!"

There! It was out. Nothing could ever be as bad again. But one of the astonishing things about Ernest was that he had no personal resentments.

"A bore? Oh, my dear, how? Do tell me."

"With all that royal genealogy. Nobody wanted such a dose."

"I *am* sorry, dear."

"Never mind being sorry. Learn not to do it again. All you have to do is behave as you do in court. You'd never have dreamt of boring a jury with all that folderol."

Ernest became silent, thoughtfully silent. But if he had been hurt, he never showed it. And from that night he almost ceased to be a bore.

8 So that was it. Some people's whole lives are told in the single episode that got them off to a good — or a bad — start. In my case it was decidedly a good one. Ernest was to continue to have periods of depression in the next four decades, but none lasted more than six or seven months, and I learned just the point when to insist, very firmly, that he quit the office and go with me to a Caribbean island or similar rest spot for the quiet and solitude that he needed. Despite these absences, ordinarily injurious if not fatal to the career of a trial lawyer whose year is studded with due dates, he managed to rise to the top echelon of the partnership. For when Ernest was at his best, there was no man at the bar who could surpass him, and I induced him to develop a loyal team at the office who could carry on if he chanced temporarily to fail. He had wondered at times if his temperament and personal difficulties were not more suited to a life of legal scholarship and teaching, but I was always convinced that his peculiar genius was for the courtroom, and surely his record has borne me out. Every law student must know of his brilliant arguments before our supreme tribunal on the great constitutional issues of the day, and indeed, had it not been for FDR's need of rubber stamps to save his New Deal legislation from conservative justices, I have little doubt that Ernest would have been appointed to the Court.

It should be obvious from the above that Ernest himself constituted my principal career. I have had no regrets about that. There was no comparison between our intellects, and what could I have done better than cope with the impediments to his? As he himself once told me, happiness is a fleeting thing, and he and I managed to get something of a grip on it. I had the time, too, to give proper supervision to the bringing up of our two children, Daniel and Ellen, though they are both today rather grudging in their acknowledgment of this. I have noted that many of the children of my friends find it fashionable to claim that they were raised by butlers and maids and saw their parents only when allowed to give them a peck of a kiss good night on the latters' way out, in swishing evening dress, to some stylish dinner party. I suspect that there may be a bit of snobbishness in this, a desire to show the world what swells the old folks were. Actually, Ernest and I went out very little at night, and I made a point of being home every afternoon at five to read to or play games with the children before their supper.

I have spoken of what I did for Ernest. He did even more for me. He gave me the confidence in myself that I had so sorely needed. After our marriage I no longer considered myself dowdy. I did what I could with such looks as I had, dressed simply but well and took pains to keep my figure. I think I looked quite as smart as most of my friends at the Murray Hill Club, though Ellen wouldn't think that much of a standard. And Ernest encouraged me to *do* things. It was with his backing and legal help that I, as president of my club, embarked on the long campaign of fund-raising for the new building, arranged for the architect and construction contract and supervised the actual work. But perhaps my greatest liberation from the shadows of childhood came with the Depression. When Daddy's remnant of the Oates fortune was substantially lost, it was Ernest who picked up the pieces, put them together in a trust safe from the speculations of my father and brothers and nursed the corpus faithfully until it yielded an income on which my by then aging parents could decently live. None of the Vermeules scorned him after that!

I offer this example of how Ernest and I operated as a team, or rather not as a team, for that implies that *he* had full knowledge of what I was doing, but as a pair, one of whom had the occasional job of bolstering the other. It was in 1950, when Ernest was over sixty, but at the height of his legal powers. He had not suffered a depression for five years.

Mr. Wentworth was now in his eighties, a splendid old gentleman of snowy hair who looked, as he had been, the subject of a Sargent portrait and who was as well known as chairman of the opera board as he was as the continuing managing partner of his firm. But he was beginning to lose his memory, thought he still came to the office every day, and Ernest and I had begun to look with some apprehension at his increasing intimacy with Jared Stokes, the thickset, taciturn and (to me anyway) faintly sinister head of the corporate department.

Stokes was a man whose sole idea of the law was as the guardian angel of large companies and who saw his firm simply as their handmaiden. He had no truck with Ernest's concept of the firm as a happy family of devoted and honorable professionals and saw no reason that new specialized partners of not necessarily high character should not be brought into the firm as the practice might need from month to month, regardless of the effect of such a policy on clerks who had given their all to Wentworth & Bailey in the expectation of seeing no rivals other than those they had started out with.

Not only had Mr. Wentworth always shared Ernest's view of the firm; he had inspired it. But now he appeared to be increasingly swayed by Stokes, whose office was adjacent to his and who lunched with him two or three times a week. I have often noted that the first creeping approach of senility may be accompanied by an almost childish spitefulness, quite uncharacteristic of the aging person's younger years, a sly wish to make trouble between the younger men who are taking his place. Ernest had always been Mr. Wentworth's favorite, but now the old man seemed to derive an actual pleasure in slighting him.

Things came to a horrid head one night when Ernest came home, very tired, and told me that he was thinking of retiring.

"Stokes wants to take Mr. Wentworth's place as managing partner. And the old man seems to favor it. Of course, it has to be put up to the firm. But Stokes appears to have a definite following among the younger partners."

"But what about *you?*"

"I'm afraid Stokes has been working on them. I shouldn't be surprised if he's persuaded them that I lack the nervous stability for the job."

"The toad!"

"Yes, but he may well be right. And I've always detested administrative responsibility. What I wanted was a five-partner committee to run the firm, with an annually rotating chairman."

"And that's not to be?"

"Not if Stokes gets his way."

"Well, maybe he won't."

"What are you plotting, Alida? I know that look."

"Never you mind."

I had prepared myself for these "retirement crises" — with Ernest's conscientiousness they came up not infrequently — by making a point of knowing, not only the wives of all twenty partners in the firm, but those of the sixty associates. It was I who had organized the annual "wives' tea," the biannual partners and wives' dinner and the New Year's Day eggnog party for all the firm. And needless to say, I had not overlooked Lita Stokes, the large, cheerful, ebullient and rather vulgar wife of the awful Jared who was reputed to be the only person in the world he feared.

I knew that Lita's greatest desire in life was to become a member of the Murray Hill Club, and I had already decided to propose her, as a way of making her an ally and neutralizing her spouse. But I had run into considerable opposition, largely because she had made her wish to join so clear. The one thing "society" cannot endure is a climber who reveals too openly that he is climbing. Lita naïvely believed that people were not afraid to face their own true motives, and she was far too candid about her own. She would talk, for example, about how she and Jared had had to drop a clinging group of old friends from an unfashionable suburb after they had moved into the city and risen in the world, as if everyone would understand the necessity of this. And she would contrast the "social positions" of her acquaintances as openly as she might have their hats. For her all the world wore its heart on its sleeve.

My position as president came near to ensuring the election of any candidate I proposed, but not altogether. I had to use a subtle tactic with Lita. I played her up to my friends as a social phenomenon, the only completely honest woman I knew.

"Lita, after all, is only saying what the rest of us are thinking. People *do* sometimes have to see less of their old neighbors as they move up the ladder. And a lot of us *do* care about social position, though we'd rather bite our tongues off than admit it. And which of us has never cultivated a rich friend for a mercenary purpose, even if it's for charity? And if we're going to be really honest, don't we have to admit that, deep down, we're a bit awed by great rank or wealth? Wouldn't we rather be asked to dinner by a duke than a poet? That's the thing about Lita. She speaks from the heart. I'd like to freeze her and put her in a time capsule so future generations would know what we were *really* like."

It had begun to work, and I had already told Lita that I was ready to propose her name. But now I called her up on the morning after my talk with Ernest and asked her to lunch with me at the club. I wanted her to be surrounded with the bliss to which she was looking forward so confidently.

"Do you know that Ernest is actually talking about retiring?" I began, in a tone which suggested that it was no great matter. After all, he *was* sixty.

"Really? But I suppose he wants to write or teach. Any law school would grab him, I'm sure."

"It's not that. It's something at the firm that's bothering him. Some absurd dispute with Jared about a committee. Can't men be ridiculous?"

"You mean about the running of the firm?"

"Something like that. It's a question, I believe, of whether Jared should be stuck with all the dirty work or whether that should be left to a committee."

Lita's round face and black eyes were coalesced into an expression of wonder.

"And Jared *wants* that?"

"So I gather."

"Well, he's always been a glutton for work. But why does Ernest care so much?"

"Oh, because Ernest has always been a fussbudget. I'd be glad to have him out of the grind, really. He'd be able at last to write 'that book,' or whatever it is. But the boring part is that I'm afraid you'll have to get someone else to put you up for the club."

Lita's small pinched lips opened into a surprisingly large hole. "Oh, no! Oh, Alida, why?"

"Well, I can't very well take the public position that you and I are such friends when our husbands aren't, can I? It would make it look as if I thought Ernest was making a fool of himself over nothing. Which he may well be, but it's hardly up to me to rub it in. It might be enough to trigger off one of his depressions."

Lita thought for a moment and then nodded grimly. "Promise me one thing. Don't do anything about the club membership until I've talked to Jared."

Years later, when I told Ellen about this, during an argument we were having about the roles that women played or didn't play in the lives of the husbands of my generation, she retorted that her father might have had a fuller life as a legal scholar had I not "maneuvered" him into remaining a trial lawyer so that I could be the wife of a rich and important partner in Wentworth & Bailey and get back at last at the scoffing Vermeules.

Really, there have been times in my life when I have almost disliked my own daughter.

The Stoic

1

I can hardly remember a time in my early life, back toward the turn of the century, when I did not worship Lees Dunbar. No doubt many other boys in New York City, or even along the eastern seaboard, felt the same way, for his power as the founder of Dunbar, Leslie & Co., the putter-together of corporate empires, the advisor to presidents, drew daily to his desk the troubled magnates of Wall Street to pour out their problems as he expressionlessly listened, examining rare stamps through a magnifying lens. Detached, Olympian, stern, he was, without a rival, my ideal of a man.

I will admit that he did not look like a great man. He was stout, with a large square face and brow topped by short thick grey hair, one lock of which curved over his forehead like a small breaking wave. His habitual expression was one of barely contained irritation, either at you or the weather, the latter seeming always somehow oppressive, as if prompting him to tear open his collar or throw off his jacket. His voice had an unpleasant rasp, and was never wasted on small talk. He was a man who needed neither friends nor relatives; his wife was a semi-invalided recluse and they had no children. It was assumed that his mind, his stamps and his art collection were all the companions he needed.

He had been a Southerner, a Virginian of gentle birth, who had come north after the Civil War, but who had not fought in it. He had gone to work for a Manhattan banker, his uncle-in-law, whose daughter he had married and whose business he had splendidly multiplied. If he had had sympathies for the Old South, he never betrayed them; it was not his way to manifest the least religious, patriotic or philosophic affiliation. His faith in money as the circulating blood to sustain an otherwise presumably purposeless humanity seemed his only creed.

Socially his life was confined to excursions on his steam yacht, the *Magellan*, and to my mother's salon. Of the latter he was the principal adornment, sitting aside in a corner armchair to which she would bring up those guests, one by one, whom she deemed sufficiently interesting in politics, finance or art to merit a few words with him. If he was in one of his gruffer moods, she would leave him alone to read his book and sip brandy.

On one such occasion I brought myself to his attention by taking a seat opposite him and also immersing myself in a book. The year was 1902; I was fourteen.

"What are you reading, George?" he asked me. "You seem absorbed." I held up *The Story of the Medici*, and he grunted. "Is it for school?"

"No, it's for me. I like to read about men who get ahead with their brains. I've never been much at games and sports."

"That rheumatic fever you had? But you're all over that, aren't you? You look pretty hale to me. A bit skinny, perhaps."

"Oh, I'm all right. But if I'd lived in Italy in those days, I doubt I'd have been much of a warrior."

"You could have gone into the Church. Become a cardinal. They ruled the roost then. Scarlet robes. Marble palaces. Poison. A good enough show. You might even have been pope."

"But didn't they have to fight, too? Didn't Julius II lead his troops into battle?"

"Only because he wanted to."

"But to be a priest." I wrinkled my nose. "Would you have cared for that, sir?"

"I?" The bushy eyebrows soared. "Not in the least. I've never said a prayer in my life."

"Nor have I. Or one I really meant, anyway."

For a moment he actually looked at me. "You might have been an artist. They were treated as equals by the great Lorenzo himself."

"But I could never draw! Even one of those square houses with a balloon of smoke coming out of the chimney."

I had made him smile. "I suppose you're trying to tell me you'd have been a banker. Well, that's a good thing to be. That book of yours should tell you how the Medici started as pawnbrokers, but succeeded in marrying into every royal house in Europe."

"I know. And it's my one ambition to become a banker. Do you think I could ever get a job with you?"

But this was precipitate. The great man returned to his book. "Work hard at school, my boy. Get to the top of your class. And when the time comes, we'll see."

I was not again guilty of such rashness in the years that followed. I continued to see Mr. Dunbar on his visits to our house and would ask him about any financial matters mentioned in the newspaper in which he had been involved. At times, finding me attentive and instructed, he would answer at some length. He noticed, too, that I never forgot a name, a date or a figure that he mentioned. At last he invited me to work as an office boy for a summer, and I had the tact never to speak to him while on the job. The following summer I was rehired and promoted to the file room. A third summer

I was an assistant cashier. By the time I had graduated from my day school (my fever had exempted me from the rough and tumble of boarding institutions), I knew as much about private banking as many adult practitioners.

At Columbia I elected courses entirely in economics and history. I became a work hound with few friends, serious youths like myself who were more concerned with figures and statistics than what some people call life. But I think I had an artist's joy in converting the hash of economic competition into the chaste black and white of a balance sheet.

My relations with Mr. Dunbar had now reached the point where I could confide in him. I don't know even today if he and I ever really "liked" each other in the ordinary sense of that vague term. I needed him, and he came in time to need me. We had the closeness of trust, the word that was the keynote of his existence. He would only do business with men whom he trusted, or purchase works of art in whose authenticity he was convinced, or have social relations with people he knew would not lie to him.

Our important conversation occurred when I was nineteen and had been invited for the first time to lunch with him in the dark tapestried downtown office that he had filled with glinting objects of gold and silver — reliquaries, platters, ewers, ciboria — all paying seeming tribute to the illuminated portrait by Zurbaran of an ecstatically praying monk. It was only on canvas that prayers invaded Mr. Dunbar's ambiance. I put to him my vital question as soon as our brief meal was concluded.

"How much longer, sir, should I go on with college? Is a Columbia degree really worth two more years of courses? I've taken all the ones I want."

"I never took a degree myself. Any man of first-class intellect is going to be his own educator. Good teachers, even great ones, are for the less intelligent. That's their function, though they'd die before admitting it. They like to boast that they 'inspire.' But the men I'm speaking about are already inspired. Did Shakespeare need a professor? Did Napoleon? Did Lincoln?"

"But I could certainly learn from you, sir."

"That would not be school. That would be apprenticeship. A totally different affair."

I turned away so that he might not see that I had closed my eyes. Then glancing at the monk, I *did* offer a silent prayer. "And when can I start that apprenticeship?"

"Tomorrow, if you're ready."

"I'll be here at eight!"

And I was wise enough to depart without another word.

My parents expressed a rare surprise when I informed them of my decision that night. They even exchanged a rather startled glance.

"Mr. Dunbar thinks so little of college degrees?" my father asked.

"He certainly thinks he can teach me more about banking than they can at Columbia."

Another glance was exchanged across the dinner table. It was Mother, as usual, who settled the issue.

"Well, if Mr. Dunbar is really going to look out for George . . ." She clasped her long hands together, the tips of her index fingers touching her lips. "Well, I really don't see how the boy could do much better."

It is time to speak of Dora and Albert Manville.

Mother's "beauty," like everything else in her life, was the product of careful planning, a major part of which was its concealment. One had to live with her to be aware of the rare hum of hidden wheels or to catch the even rarer flicker of exhaustion in the mild stare of her eyes. She knew perfectly how to make a dramatic contrast between rest and motion. The angle at which she held her head as she contemplated her interlocutor with a gently mocking air of surprise would be suddenly broken by a whoop of laughter somehow even more complimentary for being so evidently contrived. Her vivid gestures — clapping her hands or covering her face — her high silvery tones and throaty chuckles offered the continuous pantomime of a dainty romping with accepted values, a mincing two-step with the down-to-earth. Mother's small delicate nose, her rosebud of a mouth, her oval chin and high pale brow seemed almost doll-like until one recognized them as stage properties out of which a good deal of highly visible drama could be made.

Our sober little brownstone on East Sixtieth Street exploded into an elegant Elsie De Wolfe interior of bright chintzes whose chairs and divans seemed always waiting for callers and whose pillows appeared to be plumped up by invisible hands every time they were creased. My sister Eleanor and I were part of the decor, washed and combed and reclad whenever we came in, flushed and rumpled, from school or exercise. Mother treated us with a rather studied affection even when we were alone with her; her "darlings" and "pets" had a faintly theatrical ring, but, though she never lost her temper, there was a quiet ineluctability about her discipline that we knew could never be got around. Mother's children, like her furniture, had to be ready for the maid coming in with a card on a silver tray and her rising to greet a caller with: "How angelic of you to come! I was just hoping that might be your ring!"

Father to the world must have seemed the immaculate club gentleman of the era, with smooth prematurely white hair, pointed grey goatee, long handsome brown face and large aquiline nose. But his light blue eyes were windows that seemed to catch the light and reveal nothing within.

Father toiled not, neither did he spin; his days in winter were spent at the card table of his club and in summer on the golf course. His manners were ceremonious even with his children; his temper was fretted only by alterations in his routine. And it was evident even to my boyish eyes that our callers, after greeting him with the false cheer that precedes a quick dismissal, would turn their eyes at once to Mother. Not that he minded. He demanded nothing of any day but that it should be just like its predecessor.

All right, my reader will say. When is he going to come out with it? Does he think we don't *know?*

Of course, all New York knew that Dora Manville was Mr. Dunbar's mistress. The affair had been going on for years, and I'm sure there were those who fancied a resemblance between myself and the great banker, though in most respects we were physical opposites. My parents were regular members of the cruises on the *Magellan* where Mother, in the absence of the always ailing Mrs. Dunbar, acted as unofficial hostess. But the proprieties were at all times strictly observed on each side; no terms of endearment were employed, nor any fond or even affectionate glances exchanged. Father played cards and fished with his host; indeed, the only hint that anything was out of line might have been that Mr. Dunbar, never known for his tolerance of lesser men, treated this guest with a marked respect.

It was not, however, the old French convention that society should ignore what a husband chose to overlook that kept the Manhattan moralists at bay. *They* would never have considered themselves foreclosed by so mean a thing as a *mari complaisant*. No, it was the simple power of Lees Dunbar to make or break a man in Wall Street that induced them to accept his offered bribe of the rigid observance of forms. The more holy could thus pretend they didn't know;

the less sanctified had the release of gossip. The affair had the respectability we read about in Saint-Simon of the liaison between the aging Sun King and Madame de Maintenon.

I don't know when I learned of the affair first, but it seems to me I had always known. Had I gone to boarding school, it might well have been flung in my face, but at my academy, where I attended only morning classes, the boys were more tactful or perhaps more ignorant. And then we were always accompanied; in the park and at dancing school there were governesses, and in our military drill at the armory no chatter was allowed. Sex, if not gossip, I learned about in huddles in school corridors and visits upstairs in the homes of other boys. It squeezed itself into our upholstered life, and the usual first question in a boy's mind, "You don't mean Mummie and Daddy do *that?*" framed itself in mine with respect to Mother and Mr. Dunbar.

But he was old, it may be objected, old and stout and ugly. Still, he was dominating, an obvious power. In my fantasies Mother began to play the role of a white slave who had to strip and wave her hips and roll obscenely on a tiger-skin rug before the pale stare of the sultan. As I became more educated in the ways of sex, thanks to the dirtier-minded of my school associates, I pictured her doing all kinds of lewd things to whet the appetites of her jaded lord, her eyes darkening with the dark pleasure of her humiliation. I certainly felt no urge to defend her. She was a whore! A stylish whore who was earning her keep.

Eleanor, two years my senior, was a large, emotional and rather violent girl, obsessed with the snooty little clique of fashionable females who dominated her class at Miss Chapin's School, and she made little effort to conceal what a poor thing she found in me. When she finally discovered Mother's liaison (she was devoid of imagination and had to learn it from a friend), she was appalled.

"I intend to get married as soon as I possibly can," she announced to me in a storm of tears. "Of course, I shan't marry without falling in love, but I'm going to make a point of doing that with the first eligible man that comes along."

"I'd say you got there some time back," I sneered. Eleanor got from me what she usually gave. "Though the eligibility will come as a relief. Last year we thought you were going off with the piano tuner. The one who said you had a touch like Liszt. I hear he's been committed."

She didn't deign to retort. "Seriously, George, I can't stand what's going on. I don't want to live in this house a day longer than I have to."

"If you feel that strongly, why don't you go now?"

"And do what? Beg in the streets? Or worse?"

"Surely one of the aunts will take you in."

"Never. I'd have broken the sacred rule of looking the other way. The holy family commandment of sweeping it under the Aubusson. Every door would be slammed in my face."

"But nobody cares that much."

"Nobody cares at all! That's the trouble."

"Why can't you just let things be? It's not hurting you, is it?"

"That our mother's a kept woman! Does that mean nothing to you? Don't you know who pays for this house? For all the parties she gives? For your and my school bills?"

"Well, so long as they're paid." I shrugged, thoroughly enjoying now my newfound sophistication and her fury at it.

"Well, if that isn't the limit! Splashing about in the dirty puddle of your mother's dishonor! Honestly, George, I never thought even you'd be such a creep."

"Can the big talk. What are you doing but sitting on your backside in that same puddle until some fool of a guy is crazy enough to pick you out of it?"

For a moment I thought she was going to be sick to her stomach. Her face turned dark. "You crummy little bastard!" she almost shrieked. Then she paused as if hearing her own word. "Oh, my God, I'll bet it's just what you are."

"Doesn't that put you in the same boat?"

"No! He didn't even meet Mother until I was one."

"Well, you can have Father all to yourself, then. You're more than welcome to my share of him."

I guess we were both startled at where we had suddenly come out. Eleanor stared at me in mute amazement for a moment and then hurried from the room. We didn't speak of the subject again. Indeed, she and I made a point of not finding ourselves alone together. We seemed to have tacitly agreed on a kind of armed truce.

But I didn't really believe that I was Mr. Dunbar's son; Mother never seemed to me like a person to whom embarrassing accidents happen. And I shouldn't have minded if I had been. I had matured early in a household where it was evident that a child would have to take care of his own happiness and welfare. If a side had to be taken, it seemed ridiculous not to pick the stronger. Father was all form and outward show; Mr. Dunbar was life and power. If Father chose to accept his degrading position, why the devil should I object? What debt did I owe him, or even Mother for that matter? And as for my honor, how was that concerned? Was *I* sleeping with Mr. Dunbar? Could I have stopped my mother from sleeping with him had I tried? And as for the money, Father *did* have an income sufficient to feed, clothe and school me, which the law anyway required of him. *I*, then, was not legally living off Mr. Dunbar. What did Mother's diamonds (discreetly small, by the way) have to do with me? Did *I* wear them?

2   It was probably significant that when I went to work for Mr. Dunbar, he suggested that I move from home to a small but pleasant bachelor's apartment in one of the brownstones that he owned across the street from his own mansion to protect his sunshine against a possible high-rise. This might have been to make me more available for the nocturnal business conferences frequently held in his library, but I had a notion that he wanted me in a drawer distinctly separate from the one in which he kept my mother. There was to be no overlapping there, and indeed I agreed, for I had already resolved that my relation to my new boss was going to be as important to him as hers had ever been. Her appeal was to his lustful old body, but mine was to his mind, and time as well as his own innate sense of values was bound to be on my side.

From the beginning of my permanent employment with the firm I worked only for the senior partner. In the course of three successive summer jobs I had pretty well mastered the routine of the back rooms, and I was now ready to act as his "snoop," as he liked to call me, in poring through the books of companies in which he had or sought to have an interest. After only two years of this apprenticeship, when I was still a mere twenty-one, he began to send me as his emissary to interview corporate executives. He knew now that he could trust me to be properly modest and to seem as little as possible the "arrogant kid genius" that these gentlemen, however polite to the great Dunbar's emissary, undoubtedly dubbed me once the door had closed behind me.

He was not a patient man, and I saw to it that he never had to tell me anything twice. He preferred silence while he was developing plans, and I never interrupted at such times. He liked my speed and my ruthlessness in cutting out irrelevant detail. He appreciated the fact that I could change the subject from work the very moment I saw he was tired, and although I was not educated in art, I was in history and could talk easily on the historical associations of the pictures in his collection. He would sometimes even seek my advice as to a proposed purchase. After all, his collection formed a substantial portion of his wealth. Yet beyond finance and art and the occasional tales of his great business coups, we had few topics of conversation. But then had he with anyone else? Even here I could be a convenience; when it was time to put the little "genie" back in the bottle, the little genie went home.

My early and even rather dramatic preferment did not arouse as much envy in the office as might have been supposed. I think it was because my case was too special. I had not come up through the ranks; I had suddenly appeared, as Ariel on Prospero's island. It was true that I had worked those summers, but then my status had been so low that only the humblest members of the staff had been aware of me. And then it was in my favor that I had not beaten anyone out for my particular position. Mr. Dunbar had never had a young "favorite" before. Perhaps the firm considered me a first faint harbinger of the boss's senility.

Did we like each other, my old man and I? I still keep

asking myself that. Was he a surrogate father? I don't think so, really. It was more that I *was* Lees Dunbar, or a small portion of him, anyway. When I followed him down a corridor to a corporate gathering or sat behind his chair at the long conference table, I felt a tingling pride simply to be coupled with him. Perhaps I was not unlike a mystic identifying himself with his deity. In a curious fashion my ego, at what some might have deemed its grossest period, may have virtually ceased to exist.

I saw my parents very little. Mother seemed perfectly willing to accept my excuses of constant toil at the office, and Father, who surely had guessed by now that I knew all, must have been glad to be free of the embarrassment of my presence. And Eleanor, who had still not found "Mr. Right" to deliver her from a household of shame, had to loathe me for having been the confidant of the plan she had been unable to implement.

But the time was coming when my break with home would be absolute. One night in Mr. Dunbar's library, when we had concluded our discussion of a railroad receivership and I had risen to take my leave, he waved a hand towards the drink tray.

"I want to know what you think of that Van Dyck."

On the easel before the empty grate of the grey stone fireplace reclined the huge portrait that he was presumably thinking of buying. It was his custom, detested by art dealers, so to display for weeks the current candidate for his collection, nor did he hesitate to invite other dealers in to offer their opinions as to merit, authenticity and even asking price. The canvas before me depicted a young Cavalier with a wolfhound. The youth, lace-collared, long-legged, high-heeled, one hand casually on a hip, the other muzzling the affectionate canine, had high cheekbones, long blond hair and blue eyes serenely reflecting the security of his rank and station. One felt that he would have been absolutely charming to inferiors. But they would have certainly been inferiors.

"He was killed by the Roundheads in the Civil War." Dunbar slowly lit his cigar. "You can see that, can't you? He has that look of doom. But I doubt he much cared. He wouldn't have regretted a world where a brute like Cromwell could cut off King Charles's handsome head."

"I *do* feel it," I replied with some surprise, examining the picture more closely. "You might even call it 'Portrait of a Lost Cause.' "

He nodded. "And lost causes have their charm. Or don't you agree?"

I studied the canvas for another silent period. What did he want me to say? Could he have supposed that I might derive some instruction from a contrast between the young peer and myself? I too was long and skinny and of a pale complexion, but my eyes were closer together and my brown hair rose in a billow over my high brow. Mother used to say, in her mocking way, that if I hadn't dulled my eyes by squinting at figures, I might have had the air of a poet, a kind of emaciated Yeats, and saved myself the trouble of becoming a banker by courting a newly rich heiress not yet converted to society's love of the athlete. And as I thought of all this, I felt a tug at my heart. Was the Cavalier laughing at me? Or was he sneeringly suggesting that I was a kind of renegade Cavalier who had perversely turned myself into a quill-behind-the-ear Roundhead? But I didn't want to cut off anyone's head, least of all a king's. Was he too much of an aristocrat to see that I hadn't had an alternative to be anything but what I was? I turned back with something like defiance to my boss.

"Lost causes have not been exactly *your* forte, sir."

He sniffed. "Such a preference would hardly have recommended me as a guide to investors. Not that I haven't made a good thing out of *seemingly* lost causes. That's when you pick them up cheap. But the truly lost cause, the hopeless battle doomed from the start, has always had a certain attraction for me. The fact that there's nothing in it for its defenders. Nothing whatsoever. Nothing. So unlike *our* trade, my friend. Yours and mine. Yes, I think I shall acquire the Cavalier."

"Were *you* ever tempted to join a lost cause, sir?"

Ah, that was it; that was what he had wanted me to ask! He sat up. "I *was* tempted. And my whole life has turned on my successful resistance to that temptation. It was the lost cause of the Confederate states."

The pause that followed was so long that I supposed he needed a cue. "You moved north after the war, did you not, sir? From Virginia?"

"No, sir, I moved west. From Paris, after Appomattox. My father had been with the French mission during the war, and I had been his secretary. I was too young to fight in the beginning, but in 1863 I turned eighteen, and there was talk of my going home to join the boys in grey. Father, however, insisted that he needed me to stay on and help him. This was certainly a respectable excuse; it might even have been considered my duty. Henry Adams, on the other side, did the same thing for *his* father in London. I don't think I was ever seriously criticized for not joining the colors. But the important thing to me was that my decision to remain in safe Paris was in no way motivated by a desire to help my father or even the Southern cause. It was purely and simply that I saw that cause as irretrievably lost. I did not choose to lose a finger, much less my life, in fighting for it."

I hesitated, unsure what he wanted. "Surely that was only sensible."

"Ah, but was it *good?* Was it virtuous?"

I gaped. "Virtuous?"

"Yes. You must learn, George, something that I suspect you do not know about your old boss. That what is virtuous and what is not are very important questions to him."

"Well, why was it not virtuous? Your fighting would not have changed anything. Except that you might have been killed or even killed someone else. For no purpose. Wasn't that good?"

He stared at me so keenly that I felt it was I and not he that was being morally tested. "Then I find you're a stoic, like myself. You accept the world and its follies. That is, you seek to redress only those follies you *can* redress. Virtue does not weep over the irremediable woes of man. Virtue does not idly wring her hands."

I had my cue now. Virtue was not what the layman would at once ascribe to a great banker. Very well, we would teach him! Had the Cavalier not been an ass to die for such a fool as King Charles? "Futile virtue is like futile pain. It does nobody any good."

Mr. Dunbar seemed to frown from his great forehead down to his thick eyelashes. And how those pale eyes stared! But it was not a stare that seemed to focus on me; it simply included me in the landscape, solar fashion.

"You would not then involve yourself in a lost cause? Even if it were the lost cause of one of your parents?"

Ah, so *that* was it! "You are not suggesting, I presume, sir, that I should do anything to hurt my mother."

"On the contrary, you would be helping her. Financially, morally, even socially. I am old, George. I wish to dedicate my remaining years to peace and quiet. I even hope to become a better husband to my neglected spouse. But she has exacted that I first make a complete break with a certain part of my past."

That the major decisions of life should come without a struggle! But then was it really a major decision? I had only to be careful to make my face expressionless, my tone neutral. "I understand you, sir. I shall be your legate. There will be no trouble."

Those eyes! There seemed now to be a black spot in the center of each. To express a faint shock, perhaps, that I should be quite so ready, quite so quick? Did it mean that I had a nature too base for larger tasks? Was my willingness to be of service a flaw or a virtue? And then his low grunt of assent seemed to assert his recognition that possibly I *was* the rare bird he had been seeking for his later years, the man of his own genius and philosophy who would carry on what he had started. Anyway, he would try me. That was all I needed. It was all I had ever hoped for.

"You're not going to reproach me for my life *now*, are you?"

Mother was seated at her dressing table, brushing her hair with sharp strokes, still in her peignoir at ten in the morning. I was standing by the window. And, yes, I was playing with the cord of the shade. For I *was* nervous, despite my apparent containment. She continued now, turning to give me a glare:

"Surely even you wouldn't have the cold gall to do that?"

As I watched her features congeal and her glare harden, I had an odd sense of slipping inside her head and seeing myself through her eyes. Was I an unusually neurotic person, or had the peculiar circumstances of my home environment simply sharpened my perceptions while cooling my temper? For despite the tension of the atmosphere, the reaction of which I was primarily aware was curiosity. Were Mother and I for the first time actually communicating directly, without concern for manners or any of the usual human subterfuges needed to mask the ugliness of the ego? Might we even be able to recognize that our relationship had been reduced to the biological?

But no. Even if it was true in my case, it was not in hers. For she detested me. That was the difference. And now, taking my silence as the sign that I *did* mean to throw her past in her face, she dropped the reins on her temper.

"Who do you think paid for your school and college? For your Brooks Brothers suits and even your economics library? Do you think you'd have lived as you have on your father's skimpy trust?"

"Oh no. I am perfectly aware of what I owe Mr. Dunbar. And properly grateful. As, no doubt, is Father."

"You'll throw that in his face, too!"

"I'm not throwing anything in anyone's face. We all know the facts. Why not go on from there? It's also a fact that Mr. Dunbar wishes to discontinue his relations with you. Hadn't we better face it?"

"*We?*" Mother was on her feet now, her fists clenched. I had not known that she was capable of such a fit of temper. "Where do you come into it, I'd like to know? What are you but your mother's lover's pimp?"

"I should say my function was just the reverse."

"Ah, how you must loathe me to be so glib!"

I paused to consider this. "That might be what Doctor Freud would call the unconscious. But I'm certainly not aware of any such feeling."

"I hope, anyway, you're not going to tell me you're a loving son. And that what you're doing is for my good!"

"I'm not *doing* anything. I'm simply conveying a message.

A message you were bound sooner or later to receive. And I'm certainly not going to claim the status of a loving son. What have you ever done to make me love you?"

Even Mother seemed taken aback by this. "You don't think I've been a good mother? Haven't I brought you up well? What have you ever lacked? Have you no gratitude?"

"Why should I have? To have done any less than you did would have been to expose yourself to criticism as a parent. And appearances you have always been expert in. We *looked* like a happy family. That was the point, wasn't it?"

"No," she cried. "I cared for you as much as any mother. Until I saw you had as much love in you as a lizard. And think of all I did for you and Eleanor and even your father! He accepted my relationship with Mr. Dunbar because he knew he couldn't afford to give his wife and children all the things they needed. He loved me! And in return I made him thoroughly comfortable and never once humiliated him in public *or* in private. But *you!* Your greedy hand was out for Dunbar himself — you couldn't wait to slough me off. Well, let me tell you one thing, you cool young man. If you think you're going to slide into fame and fortune by posing as Croesus' bastard, allow me to assure you that, dislike it as you may, you *are* your father's child. And the great Dunbar is well aware of it!"

But, after all, I had never really believed anything else. And Dunbar would not have been a man to push a natural child, any more than he would have pushed a legitimate one, beyond, that is, a decent provision. No, he was like a Roman emperor, more apt to rely on adoption than generation to obtain the ablest successor. He had no faith in things not under his direct control. And as to what Mother had said about Father, I deemed it the merest twaddle. He had simply, in his own economic interest, known where not to look and what not to hear. But it was interesting that a woman so clear about her goals and how to achieve them should feel the need of crassly sentimentalizing two lives dedicated to simple self-aggrandizement.

It was time anyway to put an end to the discussion.

"I shall tell Mr. Dunbar that we have had this clarifying chat. And you can be sure that the easier you make the implementation of his decision, the more fruitfully will he supervise your account."

Mother's stare had now the quality of near disbelief, almost of awe, as if she were confronted with a creature of nonhuman quality. At last she emitted a hard, jarring laugh. "So I am to find virtue more profitable than vice? Oh, do get out of here before I vomit!"

I left, confident that her innate good sense would dictate a moderate course and that her wrath against me had deflected much of her ire against Dunbar. And so it worked out. We met only a few times after that, but she accepted an income from Dunbar, and after his death from me, as the least an unfaithful lover and ungrateful son could offer.

Now many if not most readers at this point will assume that I have bad character, or perhaps no character at all. I am only too well aware that many men with whom I have done business through the years, and even some of my own partners, have regarded me as a cold fish who cares for nothing but making money. Nor would the fact that I have shown little interest in spending alter their opinion, as American self-made men are notoriously more concerned with wealth than with what it can buy. Nobody, I am afraid, has ever given me credit for being, in my own way, a consistent idealist. Of course, it is true that I have never advertised the fact.

Let me summarize the aspects of my youth which *might*

have turned me into the man so many have deemed me to be. I was raised by parents who did not love me and for whom I had no respect. I had a sole sibling who detested me. An early illness kept me from being sent to a boarding school where at least I might have escaped the unsavory atmosphere of my home. And finally, I found no one around me to admire and emulate until I went to work for Mr. Dunbar.

What saved me — for I insist that I *was* saved — was my clarity of vision. I *saw* the world I lived in. I saw perfectly that it contained, outside my own family, love and honor and innocence and that it was not my fault that my life was barren of these qualities or that my heart did not beat at the pace that others liked to believe theirs did. Nor did I resent or even much envy persons more richly endowed with the gift of love. The id may be called on to rebut me here, but we cannot deal practically with the unconscious. What I was conscious of was that I had to play the hand of cards I had been dealt and that it would be futile and even ridiculous to waste my life lamenting that it did not contain more honors.

I have always been dedicated to the concepts of order and restraint in the governance of human affairs. Most of the problems of civilization, in my opinion, emanate from messy thinking and sloppy or sentimental feeling. Even Mr. Dunbar allowed his passions to embroil him in a sordid affair from which he was rescued only by the sexual impotence of old age. But he always yoked his ambition to the chariot of virtue. His life goal, he maintained, was to impose a balanced budget on a fevered and reckless world, though only if and where it was feasible. He took no credit for spreading ineffective sentiment over barren soil. Only results counted to him. And to me.

To have or not to have a loving heart is not a matter of choice but of birth. Yet people tend to applaud "warmth" and to condemn "coldness" in a man's nature as if such things were matters of merit. But merit, I insist, should attach only to what a man contributes usefully to the welfare of his fellow beings. Vain efforts, good intentions, mean nothing. That has been my credo, as Mr. Dunbar has been my god.

3 There was a change now, hard to define but nonetheless perceptible, in my relations with Mr. Dunbar. It might have been expected that we should have become more personal in our conversations, but that was not quite it. It was more that we seemed tacitly to acknowledge that we had no further secrets from each other, or at least that he had none from me. I presumably had no secrets at all. The awe, at any rate, that I constantly felt for him when out of his presence I was now able to shed at the door of his office or study. I was at ease with him alone, though this ease, if a sense of it was conveyed to him at all, must have been through some barely visible relaxing of my reserve, never of course through any idle chatter or impertinent lounging. And he, for his part, would utter his thoughts openly in my presence, almost as if I were a recording instrument for possible memoirs.

I was now invited regularly to come across the street to take breakfast with him and Mrs. Dunbar. The morning repast was her one regular appearance of the day; she still spent most of her time in her bedchamber. I was somewhat surprised to find her a dear little old lady, soft, gentle and rosily round-faced, who wore a white cap and a black silk dress in perpetual mourning for a long-dead only child. She would fuss over my not eating enough and warn me, if it was a cold day, to wear a muffler to the office.

But she also worried about my working too hard. She was afraid I was having no fun, no love affairs. And she seemed particularly anxious that I should appreciate the man behind the tycoon in her husband, perhaps suspecting me of being one of those for whom the pedestal obscures the statue.

One morning, anyway, when her husband had abruptly quit the table to take his coffee cup to his library, protesting gruffly that she was spoiling his breakfast with her constant nagging him for her little charities, she offered me this mitigation of his conduct.

"You hear, George, how he grumbles. Yet I never have to wait later than noon before a messenger brings me a check for double what I asked for. I know you young men admire him for his brilliance in business. But what I admire him for is the greatness of his heart. He is basically the kindest and gentlest of men."

I didn't quite like this. I fancied a note of denigration. Mr. Dunbar to me was a man above the world because he was free of the weaknesses that beset mankind: love and hate, pity and cruelty, sentimentality and meanness, religiosity and mendacity, holiness and vice.

"I confess I have not always found him kind and gentle. Nor do I believe that to be his general reputation downtown. No one disputes that he is a great man. But great men are not apt to be gentle."

She regarded me smilingly as if pleased to have kindled the mild impatience of my retort. "Oh, you young men today fancy yourselves such a self-contained lot. What are you afraid of? Wasn't President Lincoln a gentle man?"

"The man who unleashed the slaughter of the wilderness campaign? Hardly!"

"That he could bring himself to do *that* was part of his greater humaneness. It was for an ultimate saving of lives. Yesterday my husband promised me to do something very much against his wishes, and even against one of his old principles, to spare anguish to some persons I love. Never has he shown more tenderly what his deepest feelings have always been for me and mine."

I really sat up now. "Mrs. Dunbar, would you mind telling me what that was?"

But her eyes glistened with sudden tears. "Someday, George. Someday perhaps. Not now."

I left the breakfast table as soon as I decently could and took the subway downtown. In my office I found my throat and tongue so dry I had to drink a glass of water. Then I told my secretary I was to be disturbed by no one (Mr. Dunbar always excepted), closed my door and resumed the inspection of certain papers on my desk that I had left unfinished the night before.

They involved a trust of which Oliver Lovat was the sole trustee for his considerably richer wife. Lovat, a nephew of Mrs. Dunbar, owed his limited and very minor partnership in Dunbar, Leslie & Co. to the fact that he was the grandson of the uncle for whom Lees Dunbar had come to work after the Civil War. Lovat was a handsome if rather beefy gentleman dandy of the period, tweedy, mustachioed, derby-hatted and cigar-smoking, who had a joke for everyone, high and low, and a loud blowy manner that I cordially detested. He did no work for the firm of any significance and lived largely on the income and commissions of the

trust for his wife to whom he was notoriously unfaithful
and of which her father had been unwise enough to leave him
sole fiduciary.

Now it so happened that the much wronged Mrs. Lovat
had at last decided to check on her trustee and had hired an
accountant who had asked me, as the clerk in charge of
fiduciary accounts, for an appointment at the bank the following week. As a matter of routine I had examined the
books myself first, and the securities in our vault as well,
and I had been surprised to discover that a number of bonds
were missing. Of course, this did not have to mean a misap-
propriation; Lovat might have removed them for a sale. Yet
on the same day, receiving as I did the daily list of Mr.
Dunbar's personal market transactions, I noticed that he had
acquired the same bonds in the same denominations that
were missing in the Lovat trust. And now, after Mrs. Dunbar's mysterious revelation, only one interpretation fitted the
facts.

Lovat, a known gambler on the stock market, must have
hypothecated trust assets to cover his personal loans and was
now unable to replace them. Learning of his wife's proposed
investigation, he had thrown himself on his knees before his
soft-hearted aunt, and she had prevailed upon her husband
to make good the loss.

Now this was certainly a new light on my great man, nor
did I welcome the idea of any change in his iron character.
He was not simply the major influence in my life; you might
say he was the only one. I had liked to think of him as a cold
man, but only in the sense that I too was cold: reason ruled
our hearts. He was always just and fair in all his business
dealings, and his word was his bond. And now was he com-
promising his standards? The ideal of virtue he had so loftily
preached to me?

Surely this would be a relaxation of one of his greatest strengths. He had always stipulated for absolute honesty among his own partners and in his own dealings. Anyone who tried to take crooked advantage of him would never do business again with Dunbar, Leslie & Co. As with the dealers who sold him art, to be once caught in a lie was to be banished forever. He believed that American business could police itself, and he had nothing but contempt for reform politicians.

But now had the bell struck? I am still proud to say that I did not flinch before the challenge. Armed with my list of his recent market purchases, I marched into his office and laid it boldly on his desk.

He picked it up and read it slowly, as if for the first time. I was almost embarrassed for him, which made me even bolder, daring enough to put this reminder to him:

"You once asked me, sir, if your decision not to take a military part in the Civil War had been a virtuous one."

How still he was! But he might have been crouching. "Yes, sir. And, as I recollect, you told me you believed it had been."

"I was deeply impressed at how much you cared that any act of yours should be virtuous."

He nodded. "And now you are wondering how much I still care."

"Precisely."

"You have perceived that I am preparing to make whole my wife's nephew's misappropriations."

"Just so."

"And you are questioning the virtue of what I am considering?"

"No, sir, I am not questioning it. I am condemning it."

Oh, he liked that! He liked to be stood up to by one who

knew what he was doing. "Condemning without a trial? Without considering all the facts? I am saving a man's wife from destitution, our firm from disgrace, himself from indictment. And I can police him in the future. I shall require his resignation from his fiduciary position. He will be no further menace to society."

"But you will have concealed a felony. *You* will know that in the future the word of Lees Dunbar will be good only when the circumstances are propitious."

"My word, sir? What word?"

"You will be certifying to an accountant that a trust is in order."

"And will it not be?"

"Only when you have doctored it."

He grunted and now moved for the first time, shifting heavily in his chair. "Let us consider the consequences. Oliver will be a desperate man. He may even do himself in. He's just the type that does. Where will be the benefit to society?"

"Is that our criterion?"

"We? Are 'we' so sure of our own motives? You, for example. Mightn't my nephew offer a possible obstruction to your own advancement in the firm? 'The old boy is getting senile,' my partners may be already saying. 'How many protégés do we have to put up with? First the incompetent Lovat and now this young fellow with whose family the old boy had such a curious intimacy? Isn't one enough?' "

I smiled inwardly. Surely I had achieved the ultimate union with him now. That he should even speak of the "curious intimacy"! "I'm not worried about Lovat, sir. I could lick him in the firm with one hand tied behind my back."

Again that slow nod. "I believe you could. Very well.

Let us probe even deeper. Mightn't we — and I do mean
both of us — derive an actual satisfaction from the bloody
sacrifice we would be making on the altar of our given
word?"

"Should the pleasure of doing the right thing disqualify us
from doing it?"

A ponderous silence. "Why are you doing this to me,
George?"

"Because I believe in you, sir."

"And because you believe in nothing else?"

I must confess, this took me aback. "That could be in it, I
suppose."

"That's what I'm afraid of." His sigh, if deep, was final.
"Very well. Obviously, I cannot now proceed with my little
plan of rescue. But don't worry. I shall not hold it against
you. I even sympathize with your point of view. Alas! I
must tell the wretched Oliver to look elsewhere for his
salvation. What a world! But I had no hand in the making of it."

Oliver Lovat's body was fished out of the East River the
next morning. He had joined the army of those despairing
souls who elect to solve their insoluble problems by a leap
from Brooklyn Bridge. But there was no disgrace for the
firm or destitution for the widow, as the real motive for the
suicide was never discovered. His debts and disorderly love
life provided adequate causes for the journals. And it was I
who suggested to Mr. Dunbar that it would now be in order
to replace the embezzled securities before the accountant's
inspection. There was no longer an embezzler to be prose-
cuted. But I suspect that Mrs. Dunbar had somehow divined
my role. The invitations to breakfast were rescinded on the
excuse that she now took that meal in her room.

Her husband made up for the breakfasts by asking me

regularly to lunch in his office. There was nothing at this point that he did not discuss with me, from his purchase of a still life to the merger of two railroads. And at the bank I was now universally treated as the established favorite. I did not trouble myself with how much envy and how much dislike might be concealed under the polite exteriors. I knew that none of the juniors would play any part in my rise or fall. I had staked my all on Mr. Dunbar, placing my eggs in a single basket, but having total faith in the reliability of that container. He might die — but a banker must be prepared to take *some* risk.

And indeed it was not long before he advised me that the time had come for me to extend myself socially in the firm.

"We'd better start thinking about a partnership for you. Twenty-seven is young in the eyes of the world, but you have the experience of a much older man. You must become better known to the partners. We'll start with John Leslie. He will ask you for a weekend on Long Island. He won't, of course, mention that I have suggested the invitation. You will be your discreet self about that."

"Of course, sir."

"And pay some attention to his daughter, Marion. Unless your heart is otherwise engaged?"

"Free as air, sir."

"As I rather supposed. You work too hard, my boy. Marion's a fine girl. A bit on the athletic side, but handsome. Apparently she's had some sort of unhappy love affair which she claims she'll never get over. But women like to make a drama of these things. We know about that. There are two brothers in the London office, fine fellows, charming, but a bit on the playboy side. It's not a sure thing they're partnership material. Leslie might content himself with a partner son-in-law. *Verbum sapienti.*"

I restrained a gasp. Had I really come *that* far? Like a papal nephew in the Renaissance marrying into the old Roman nobility? "But would a girl like that so much as look at a dreary bank clerk who doesn't even play polo?"

He shrugged scornfully. "You don't want me to tell you *how* to do it, do you? Go to. You're not a bad-looking fellow. A bit on the skinny and pale side, but even that can be attractive. Who knows? She may be tired of the brawny brainless. And her old man tells me that she's got a thing about the firm. Wishes she'd been a man so she could be a member of it. It's up to you, my boy!"

🌸 🌸 🌸

4   Mr. Leslie was as handsome, as suave and as unsurprising as his fine, purple brick Tudor mansion with its emerald lawns and shady
🌸 🌸 🌸   elms and white-fenced fields and stables. He had thick black-grey hair, a strong, well-shaped nose, a square chin and gleaming white teeth. He had to have had brains to have achieved his position in the firm and his assistant secretaryship of the army under Theodore Roosevelt, but I supposed his mind had been largely and shrewdly focused on using a charming personality to its best advantage. Mr. Dunbar, who was plain to the edge of ugliness, had notoriously converted his envy of good-looking males to a desire to be surrounded by them; it was a distinct tribute to my own intelligence that I had become his intimate without a stalwart build.

When my weekend host offered me golf or tennis and learned that I played neither, he turned me over to his daughter with a pleasant grin that effectively masked any scorn the athlete must have felt. If a protégé of Lees Dunbar could play only tiddledywinks, then tiddledywinks it would be.

Marion, tall, broad of shoulder, with the fine paternal nose and high clear brow, but with moppy rich auburn hair, made no effort to conceal her disgruntlement at my paucity of athletic choice. I soon learned that she made no effort to conceal any of her reactions. The good things of life had been plumped into her lap where she obviously felt they belonged.

"Well, shall we put on our bathing suits and sit by the pool?" she asked. "We can lend you a suit if you don't have one."

But I had no wish to expose my etiolated figure to the contrast of her brothers' brown muscles. If she was to be won, it would not be that way.

"Why don't you take me for a walk? I'd love to make a tour of this beautiful place."

"Oh, all right." She brightened a bit. "We've got a thousand acres, you know." She glanced at my polished shoes. "Can we provide you with sneakers?"

"No, I have a pair, thank you."

And off we went across the meadows, pausing to watch grazing horses and Black Angus, into the woods to the marshland abutting Long Island Sound. Her enthusiasm waxed when she saw I didn't mind a good pace or getting my sneakers muddy when she put a finger to her lips and beckoned me to follow her for a closer look at a perched hawk. On the way back she became more conversational.

"I suppose you don't have much time for sports. Daddy says you work too hard. But that you're one of the real up-and-comers at the office."

"He flatters me. But it's true about the work. I never seem to have concentrated on games."

"You're not like most of the young men I know. You're more serious. I guess that's a good thing. But haven't you missed them? The sports, I mean."

"I don't think so."

"You don't think they're important?"

"Well, they're not to me. They're important to the wealthy, I suppose. They help kill time. You pointed out yourself that one needed time for them."

"Yes, but not just to *kill* it. I never heard such a strange idea. What *do* you find important?"

"Finance."

"You mean making money?"

"Well, that's certainly a part of it. After all, this lovely place, the horses, the cattle, the opportunities for sport, your whole life here, what does it depend on but money?"

Her nose indicated her distaste. "Mother's always taught us it's vulgar to talk about money."

"That's because our families like to think of themselves as aristocrats. They want to feel they owe their position to birth and not just dough. But they're wrong. As mine found out when they lost theirs."

Marion paused. She had not decided whether or not to take offense at my line of argument.

"You sound like a radical."

"Because I talk about money? I should have thought it was just the opposite."

"But you don't think like other people."

"Maybe that's because I think."

"You're pretty sure of yourself, aren't you?"

I decided it was time to pull up. I had made a sufficient gesture of independence. "Forgive me for being such an ass.

I'm not used to talking to attractive and intelligent young women. I'm just not socially experienced, I guess."

Marion smiled. "Oh, you're not doing so badly. We may make something out of you yet."

At dinner that night were just the family and I. I had the feeling it was a rare occasion that induced Marion's two handsome brothers, on leave from London, muscular, thin and bony, one dark and one light, like black and spotted jaguars, to sup at home without female guests. But why? Did Mr. Dunbar's arm reach even into his partners' domestic arrangements?

If so, it had failed to touch Mrs. Leslie. Her attitude towards me had none of the friendly accord of her husband and sons. She was a plain, silent, rather grim little woman who seemed to have nothing in common with her good-looking and cheerful family. She had been an heiress herself, I knew, but surely John Leslie could have made his fortune without the help of hers. Or was there, in his very shining air of assurance, the hint of a nature that would have taken *no* chances? Anyhow, the way she reduced the required acknowledgment of my presence to the briefest of nods showed what use she had for the "likes of me." I supposed she saw me as the son of a kept woman, probably as a kind of *fils complaisant*.

But the "boys," Jack and Bob, my own age, more and less, were another matter. They, like their old man, were charming. They might not have been intellectual, but they had plenty of wit for amiable small talk, and they made pleasant fun of their father and sister (never of Mama!) as they exchanged smiles and knowing glances. They were politely complimentary to me in their questions about my work, perhaps overly so. Were they laughing at me? Very likely. But there might have been another compliment to my perspicacity in their letting me see that they saw I saw it, that they counted on me to appreciate their innate good will in a world where one thing, after all, was pretty much as inconsequential as another: a game of tennis, a bond issue, a polo match, a mortgage foreclosure. It was my first glimpse of the aristocratic point of view.

I found it pleasurably warming, but it also dug an odd little crater of desolation somewhere in the root of my being. For I could never be as they, or really included by them. They shared a fraternity of looks and sports and jokes and easy masculinity of which I could never be a true part. At a later date, Bob, the younger brother, would tell me that he recognized only three types among his male acquaintance: "swell guys, shits and genial shits." He didn't say it, but I knew the only category I could aspire to was the third.

Jack, who was slightly more serious than his younger brother, brought up the subject of Mr. Dunbar's great repute.

"Dad tells us, George, that you know Mr. Dunbar better than anyone else does in the whole firm. Even than Dad. Do you consider him one of the great men of our time?"

"The greatest," I replied stoutly.

"More so than Theodore Roosevelt?"

"Even than him."

There were surprised looks around the table. Mr. Leslie, after all, had been a member of the ex-president's administration.

Mrs. Leslie now spoke for the first time. "Mr. Manville, no doubt, is speaking of financial greatness. Surely he will concede that Mr. Roosevelt is the greater *man*."

"Not even at the risk of disagreeing with my hostess."

"Aren't you forgetting an essential quality in greatness? Theodore proved himself a hero at San Juan."

Was the Christian name meant to subdue me? I was defiant. "You agree then with Brooks Adams, Mrs. Leslie?" What, after all, had I to lose? "That war and faith are the marks of a high culture? And that we live in the dark age of the goldbug?"

She looked at me now with a first flicker of interest. But it was just a flicker. "You and I, Mr. Manville, are surely the only ones of this benighted group who have read *The Law of Civilization and Decay*. Yes, I feel there's something in his theory."

But the glance that she bestowed on her sons robbed me at once of my new consideration. What could she think of a world where such a one as I might outrank two such strapping fellows?

"Lees Dunbar," she continued now in what was almost a growl, "never fought in a war. And he was of an age to have done so."

"My wife has always been a breather of fire and brimstone," Mr. Leslie intervened hastily to divert the discussion from so disloyal a turn. "She would rather have had Mr. Dunbar in uniform even if it would have put him on the wrong side!"

But I felt quite justified now to use my hostess's weapons against her. I declined his polite invitation to make a joke out of it.

"President Roosevelt's father did not fight in that war, either. And what is more, he bought a substitute."

"There you are, Ma!" Bob exclaimed. "He got you on that one!"

His father again changed the subject as his wife indignantly shook her head. I felt, perhaps unreasonably, that I had been almost a success.

When I walked again with Marion the following morning,

however, I was much less sure of this, at least as far as she was concerned. She was pensive and responded to my remarks with short replies which effectively killed each new subject offered. At last I challenged her.

"You're different today. Did I say or do something wrong last night?"

"Oh, no, not at all. You were very lively and amusing. And I know that's not so easy with a family like mine."

"But they're charming!"

"You found Mother charming?"

"Well, perhaps that's not just the right word for her. Deep persons may have little use for charm."

We had come out of the woods to a clearing in the center of which was a pile of rocks which offered inviting seats. At least they invited Marion to pause.

"Shall we stop here for a bit, George? I want to talk to you."

She seated herself on one of the higher rocks. Then she gazed across the meadow for a full minute before she spoke, very articulately and coolly, except for an occasional throb in her tone. She must have prepared her speech. Perhaps she had risen early to do so.

"I had a sense last night that Daddy and the boys were throwing me at you. Now, why should they wish to do that, you will ask. I'm not exactly the last leaf on the tree. I'm only twenty-three and certainly not ugly. No, please don't interrupt. Let me talk. What has happened is that I've been through a wretchedly unhappy time. I fell in love with a man called Malcolm Dudley. He was twenty years older than me and had a problem with drink and something of a poor reputation with women. And he had no job — only enough money for a bachelor's life of sports. Obviously not the beau that Daddy ordered. But oh, George, he had charm! Talk about birds lured from trees! And the sweetest nature in the world. And he loved me, too. He really loved me!"

I saw by the caged wildness of her eyes how fiercely that love must have been returned. I was even nearly persuaded that the wretched Dudley could not have been altogether a sham. Had he cultivated her for her fortune and been caught himself?

"He saw perfectly that he was a hopeless match. He even shed tears over the fact that he had got us both into such an emotional state. Mother said she'd rather see me in my coffin than wedded to such a man. And then Daddy killed the whole thing. He hired a detective who discovered that Malcolm had an illegitimate child by a girl in Philadelphia. Of a good family, but poor. Daddy confronted us both with this. He offered to make a settlement on Malcolm if he would marry the girl and give his child a name. Malcolm turned to me and said he would do as I told him. What choice did I have?"

What could I say to *that?* I was dumbfounded that any father could have known his daughter so well. For indeed there was a Roman quality to Marion. One could hardly imagine her in any role but the heroine.

"And *did* Dudley marry the girl?"

"He did. He agreed it was his duty. There was a terrible scene. He wept."

"He seems to have done his share of that."

"Don't malign him! He's a man of the deepest feeling."

"But what sort of marriage will his be? And if he had a drinking problem to boot . . ."

"I know, I know!" She clasped her hands in agony. "It may all be god-awful, but at least that child will have a name."

I had no need to probe further into the well-deserved purgatory of Mr. Dudley. I allowed some moments to pass in which I might have been musing on the sadness of her story. Then I asked:

"And what does all this have to do with your being thrown at *me?*"

"Well, you see, I told my family that I could never love again."

"Oh, come now."

"And I can't!" Her tone was passionate. "You must believe that!"

I shrugged. "Anyway, you convinced your family of it." I made my tone bitter. "And they decided you'd better meet a man who wouldn't mind? Who would be satisfied with other considerations? Such as money and social position, not to mention interest in the firm? And while they were at it, hadn't they better pick a comer? Possibly even a future partner?"

"Oh, George, don't," she pleaded. "I'm so ashamed. I didn't see it that way when Daddy asked you down here. It wasn't until I saw how he and the boys made up to you at dinner that I realized what was going on. Oh, please go home now — I'll take you to the train — and in the future try to think of me as kindly as possible."

It was at that moment that I may have fallen in love with Marion. That is, as much in love as my stunted nature allowed. I also saw that she was precisely the wife I needed, from every point of view I could *then* imagine. How could my clear mind not take that in? That I might, for the asking, have everything: love, position, wealth! Everything, I might have added had I not been so green, but this young woman's love.

"Let me propose something, Marion. I shall go back to

town now, as you suggest. But can we meet again with the promise that neither of us will ever mention Malcolm Dudley or your father's little project vis-à-vis myself again?"

"You like me well enough to want to do that?"

"Why don't you give me the chance to find out? There'd be no commitment on either side."

Oh, how her large brown eyes peered and peered at me! Marion knew that she hadn't fathomed me at all.

"Well, why not?" she demanded, almost wearily, at last. "What does either of us really have to lose?"

5 My courtship of Marion was a curious one. I could have asked, like Richard III, if ever woman had been that way won. It was all based on the premise that she was no longer capable of loving, that her emotional capital had been too lavishly spent on Mr. Dudley to have left more than a trickle of income to water, with a bare adequacy, any romance conjured up to avoid the aridity of old-maidhood. I did not for a minute believe that her capital had been so depleted, but it suited my purpose that *she* should believe it and that I offered the best practical solution to escaping the pity of a too loving family.

She liked, on our now regular meetings, to inaugurate serious discussions. She would even suggest a topic for each of our walks: could women be bankers; was divorce the only answer to an unhappy union; was charity demeaning to the recipient; should we get into the war in Europe. I did wish at times that she would be less blunt in facing what she deemed to be the bleak status of her emotional options. I had never before been as close as this to a young woman, and the idea of romance as a partner or even a possible competitor to my infatuation with work was beginning to titillate me. But Marion did little to enhance this feeling.

I was now invited to spend an occasional weekend with the Leslies on Long Island. Mrs. Leslie had consented to tolerate me — barely. Marion and I took long — rather too long — rambles across the countryside. She seemed never to tire and showed a preference for thick woods and even brambles over paths. When we rested — always at my request — on some rocky seat, she would not even let me take her hand in mine.

"Let us be sensible, George. We needn't go in for anything like that until we know just where we're headed."

"But where *are* we headed? You must remember, please, that *I* have not been the victim of an unhappy love affair. It's not so easy for me to be cool and detached. My heart was free. Until I met you, of course."

"I like your 'of course.'" Her mildly amused smile seemed to define the distance she had placed between us. "I see perfectly that you *want* to be in love with me. But that doesn't have to mean that you are. Or even that you ought to be. *Have* you ever been in love, George?"

"Never."

"Then maybe you never will be. And maybe that's not a bad thing. Lots of people never fall in love, I'm sure. Probably many more than is generally suspected."

"I wonder if your mother isn't one of them."

"Oh, no," she replied quickly. "I'm sure Mother's very much in love with Daddy. The shoe's on the other foot there."

She didn't pursue this interesting idea, but it struck me

suddenly that she might well be right. There could have been a coolness under her handsome father's cheer and a passion behind her plain mother's moodiness. And could *this* be why Marion was tolerating my uneasy courtship? Because she wanted a mate who would not importune her? A partner in the firm, like her father, who would be a credit to her name and not a bore about her body? And now that the horrid idea had surfaced, I had to know.

"Marion, just what is it that you have in mind? Why are you putting up with me at all?"

She met this calmly. "That's a fair question. I think we should both be weighing the pros and cons of marriage."

"But what sort of a marriage? What the French call a white one?"

She flushed slightly and looked away. She had not been quite ready yet for such candor. But she met the challenge. "Yes, do you really care? Please don't be a hypocrite, George. I have this idea that you're not a very passionate man. And what you did on the side would be no business of mine. I suppose a lot of people would think it cold-blooded that we should be having this discussion at all, but I don't really see why. Marriages have been 'arranged' throughout history. The only difference is that we'd be doing the arranging, not our parents."

"But yours, I gather, would go along with it."

"Daddy, certainly."

"And your mother?"

"Oh, one can never be sure with Mother. But at least she hasn't said she'd rather see me in my coffin, as she did with poor Malcolm."

"Thanks!"

"Well, *you* asked. You and I might be a great team in running Dunbar Leslie one day. Daddy always says that

Mrs. Dunbar and Mother didn't do their share of the social side. Well, I wouldn't be like that!"

I sighed. "And I suppose you won't even allow that love might come after marriage."

"It's better not to count on it. I *do* like you, George. I like your honesty and your seriousness. And I think we might get on very well together. There. That's enough for now. Let's walk on."

I think we both felt that matters had been accelerated by the great event that now befell me. At least a year before I had deemed it possible, I was elected a partner in Dunbar, Leslie & Co. Mr. Leslie came himself to my office to congratulate me warmly. Then he rose to close my door. Speaking in a lower tone, he added:

"And if this brings another pot to boil, you will find no objections from one John T. Leslie, Esquire."

What could a young man do but blush, jump to his feet and grasp the hand of the eminent gentleman who consented so graciously to be his father-in-law?

The flatness which I undeniably felt would surely not have been an aspect of my reaction a year before. Not having met the Leslies, I should have been as close to ecstasy as was possible for one of my temperament. But now that I had seen in them the life of the successful banker *combined* with the joys of family love and solidarity, I could recognize a fuller and more rewarding existence than any I had ever visualized. I had qualified as a husband for a Leslie, but only on a stipulated condition. Like the Byzantine general Marcian, I would be elevated to share the throne with Empress Pulcheria, but not her bed.

The prospect tarnished the glitter of my new position in the office. A membership in the firm, which had once seemed to me the peak of worldly ambition, now threatened to be a lonely rank, even (to any who suspected the truth) a shameful one. Yet, as I took new stock of my assets and liabilities, I could see no valid alternative to proceeding in the direction in which I had so long been headed. A junior partnership was one thing, but I had my eyes on becoming the senior of all, and if Mr. Dunbar should die, I would surely need the Leslies to achieve the highest rung.

When I called at their town house later that same day, Marion received me alone in the parlor. She had already heard about my partnership. Her elation seemed to be strangely mixed with a sudden misgiving.

"Are you as happy as you should be, George? There are moments when I feel that I don't really know you. I guess this is one of them."

"Oh, I'm thrilled, of course. How would I not be?"

"But would you tell me if you weren't?"

I hesitated. "Why do you ask that?"

"Don't most married couples tell each other everything?"

"Some may think they do."

"But they deceive themselves?"

"If they believe the impossible, yes."

"Wouldn't you want to know everything your wife was thinking?"

"In the name of God, no!"

There was a long, rather tense pause before she laughed. Loudly, and at last almost cheerfully. I had the sense that some lurking reservation had been thrown, perhaps recklessly, to the winds.

That evening we became engaged.

Mrs. Leslie was supposed to be as unforgiving as she was righteous. Had she ever, it was said, even once surprised her husband with a pretty housemaid on his knee, she would have left him forever. The mere apprehension of such a crisis was reputed to have kept him permanently faithful. But she seemed to have condemned me on the subject of my parents without the need of evidence. This came out in our discussions of plans for the wedding.

We met, Marion and I and her unsmiling parent, in the latter's chaste pale second-floor sitting room in the Long Island house, with its pastels of the children in their youth and its small glass bookcases filled with the leather-bound volumes of poetry which its grim occupant so unaccountably loved. Banned from its white walls was any suggestion of the trophies that her game-hunting spouse placed over the halls below. No horn, claw, tusk or antler was allowed to sully the purity of the atmosphere.

"A wedding without a single member of the groom's family is an anomaly, George." Her use of my Christian name had been her sole acknowledgment of the engagement. "It looks as if we refused to have them, which isn't true, or as if they held something very strongly against you. I'm afraid I must ask you what that is."

"Mother, hadn't you better talk to George alone?"

"Certainly not, Marion. If there *is* something, surely it's as much your concern as mine."

"But I don't *care*. I trust George for that. I don't want to know anything about his family quarrels. That's his affair. Besides, he has two aunts who will be happy to attend the wedding."

"Aunts aren't enough. Well, George? Are you going to tell us?"

Of course, I was ready for her. It would be my first important lie, but I had weighed all the circumstances, and I was convinced that I had moral justification. "It invokes delicate matters, Mrs. Leslie."

"I expected that."

"You are aware, I'm sure, of my mother's past relationship with Mr. Dunbar."

"Perfectly."

"Mother, I don't want to stay to hear this!"

"Sit down, Marion, and don't be a fool. You can't play the innocent with me. Do you think I don't know what you and your girlfriends gossip about? Go on, George."

"You can imagine that the situation was not agreeable to me. To have my mother so involved, and my father, whether from weakness or love, willing to look the other way! It made it all the worse that Mr. Dunbar, whom I worshiped, should be responsible for the degradation of my family. At last I resolved to have it out with him. I pleaded with him to break off with my mother. I went so far as to urge him never to see or even speak to her again. At first he was furious. I expected to be fired on the spot. But in the end he was too great a man not to be affected by my candor. After due consideration he decided to end the intrigue. My mother learned of my role and has never forgiven me. She has turned my father and sister against me. And she is quite remorseless. There is nothing I can do to bring her around."

Mrs. Leslie's face was a study. I wonder if she had ever been more perplexed in her life. Sexual misconduct has been pretty much the same through the ages, and society has usually been resigned to leaving it under the rug where common sense had customarily swept it. But if the dogma of a particular era requires condemnation if the rug happens to be pulled back, then all must join in that condemnation. In a Victorian or puritanical age my reasons would have been publicly accepted as the justification of my alleged interference, even by those who would have privately regarded me as a prig and a busybody. But was that true in 1916? By then my alleged sanctimoniousness might have been considered almost as low as adultery itself. But not quite. It was obvious that Mrs. Leslie found distasteful my account of the Galahad son, but her feelings would have been much stronger had she known my true role. And she was not sufficiently liberated from puritan doctrine to criticize me openly. Oh, I had her! I was no longer the *fils complaisant*. She would have to go through not only with the wedding but with the large reception that I had in mind.

As she still, however, did not speak, I urged her to check my story with Mr. Dunbar himself. This was a bold stroke. I was pretty sure that even she would lack the gall to do this, but I figured that if she did, the great man would at once deduce what I was up to and, chuckling inwardly, confirm my story.

"No, that won't be necessary, George," she replied with a sigh. "I don't doubt your word. Well, that's it, then. We'll have the wedding without the Manvilles."

6 America's entry into the Great War followed shortly upon our marriage, but there was no idea of my joining the colors. I was significantly involved in the loans to Britain, and even as fierce a war-horse as my mother-in-law had reluctantly to agree that the firm was justified in applying for my draft exemption. But Marion's brothers were both engaged as infantry officers in the trenches, and Jack, the elder and the more promising, was killed in action. When Bob re-

turned from the carnage, he had no further taste for banking, and he bought a large cattle ranch in Argentina which he colorfully and unprofitably operated thereafter at the family's willingly defrayed expense.

As I was the only relative of John Leslie's left in the firm, as well as the continuing intimate of the now sadly aging Lees Dunbar, it might have been thought that my succession to the leadership was assured, and for a time this appeared to be the case. But I could nonetheless perceive behind the faultless good manners of my father-in-law and the perfunctory civility of his spouse that the tragic events of wartime had not improved their opinion of me. The slaughtered youth at Château-Thierry and the hard-riding gaucho of the Argentine pampas had set a standard of virility that a mere economic whiz kid could never hope to attain. It may have seemed, even to the eyes of the nonrelated partners, that I had taken some obscure advantage of my gallant brothers-in-law, who in any case would have more graced the aristocratic corridors of Dunbar, Leslie & Co. than the pale creature in dark civilian garb who seemed to be thinking only of profits while his betters were dying.

Marion herself was not immune to this attitude. She had not, however, seemed to have felt it at first. Our marriage had got off to a better start than might have been expected. Her equable disposition enabled us to live together like two college roommates. She was frankly bored by my political and economic theorizing and didn't even pretend to listen if I held forth on these subjects, but she took, as she always had, the greatest interest in the social side of my business life and loved to entertain the members of the firm and their wives in the commodious houses that she built in town and country. Indeed, her father used to twit her for deeming herself the Agrippina of Dunbar Leslie, being the daughter, wife and (he vainly hoped) future mother of "emperors." I daresay some of the partners' wives thought she put on airs and scoffed at her rousing cheerleader tones, her tossed head and noisy good will, but no doubt they were careful to do so behind her back.

But the loss of Jack and the absence of Bob had, by 1920 anyway, begun to affect our relationship. It might have been because those friendly fellows were no longer around to take my side and back me up. I believe that they had always been rueful about the way they and their father had conspired to give me a loveless wife (they did not know *how* loveless) and that they kept an eye on their sister to be sure she was nice to me. But now their loss served only to remind Marion of how little I seemed a male Leslie. She never said so, but she was cooler with me, at times irritable. I suspected that she had forgotten Malcolm Dudley at last and was beginning to wonder why she had doomed herself to a *mariage blanc*.

And indeed it was not long before she appeared to be taking steps to mitigate the rigor of this doom. In Old Westbury she went fox hunting or golfing every weekend with Hugh Norman, my partner and our neighbor. Hugh, my exact contemporary, was generally considered my nearest rival in the firm. He was certainly not like me in any respect, with his strong build, his slicked-back dark hair, his long stern countenance and eyes which could somehow twinkle and reprove at almost the same time. He gave a remarkable impression of strength, both in character and physique; one suspected that he had been a polo player or something equally stylish and arduous. And to top it off, he had what the military call "command presence"; he could dominate a meeting without raising his hand or his voice. Needless to say, I detested him.

Hugh was married to a wonderful woman of great character, but Aggie Norman had been stricken with a terrible polio five years before and was confined to a wheelchair. Hugh was supposed by the office to have had occasional discreet affairs, and for a time I naïvely took it for granted that these satisfied the rutting male in him and that he and Marion were united primarily by their love of sport and their joint passion for the firm. For Hugh, quite as much as I, lived essentially for Dunbar Leslie.

I had also thought that Marion was not the type to appeal to his senses. Were not men as cold and grave as he notoriously attracted to gamier morsels? But I had underestimated the subservience of his baser appetites to his ambition. If he could subject an infatuated Marion to his will, he might dominate, through her, her adoring father — and John Leslie's share of the firm's capital was second only to Mr. Dunbar's. And if John Leslie became the trustee under Dunbar's will . . . well, what would *that* mean to the future of George Manville?

When I was fool enough to twit Marion with the rumors of her hunting companion's extracurricular sex life, she warmly defended him.

"And if it were true, what's the harm? He's a man, isn't he? Aggie Norman understands that. She and I have become the greatest friends, you know. She wouldn't want him to be frustrated. It might make him difficult in the home. It might even affect his work at the office."

"Because all that loose semen knocking around inside him might clog a he-man's business judgment?"

"George! I've never heard you be so vulgar. What's come over you?"

"Jealousy, perhaps."

"Jealousy? You can't expect me to take *that* seriously?"

Really, was it possible for a woman to be so insensitive? Even granting what our marriage was, or wasn't, couldn't she see that I might still be uncomfortable?

"While we're on the subject of Hugh, don't you think your seeing so much of him may cause people to talk?"

Her firm answer made me suspect that she had been waiting for this. "Let them. And now let me ask *you* something. Hugh and I think we ought to do even more things together. He thinks we ought to take over the firm's entertainments. The receptions, staff parties and so on. Aggie's simply too ill to do more than have a few friends for supper at home, and we all know how you've always hated any kind of office socializing."

"But haven't I always done my part?"

"Yes, dear, but *so* reluctantly. I've always had to drag you! And Hugh has a great flair for public relations. He needs a hostess, and I've always regarded the social side of business as my particular forte. So people are just going to have to get used to seeing us act as a team. I'm sure they'll come to view it as a business relationship. I assume you have no real objection?"

"None whatever," I replied bitterly. "You'll both do it to the queen's taste."

Marion wasted no time in putting her plan into effect. At office gatherings in the following months she and Hugh acted as host and hostess, and as this appeared to have the total sanction of their spouses, Aggie's illness and my solitary preferences being known, the firm seemed to accept it. At a reception at the Waldorf which the partners gave for a delegation of Japanese industrialists, I was told that they made a handsome, almost a royal, couple, receiving together at the head of the grand stairway.

But the woman who told me this, the catty wife of a

younger partner, the sort of person who would sacrifice her husband's very future for the pleasure of making a disagreeable remark, added: "One would have thought them Princess Flavia and Rudolph Rassendyl in *The Prisoner of Zenda*. So romantic!"

I realized then that I could no longer go on fooling myself. Except what would I really gain by facing the truth?

7 That same year saw a congressional committee's investigation of monopolies, and Mr. Dunbar himself was called as a witness. I accompanied him to Washington, indignant at the idea that he was being summoned, not because the testimony of an old man of now obviously declining memory would be helpful to proposed legislation, but because his famous name might provide a football to be kicked about for political advantage. And so indeed it turned out.

Mr. Dunbar had difficulty with some of the questions. He showed a vagueness as to the identity of certain corporate mergers that he could have recited in his sleep a few years before. But Rex Florham, counsel for the committee, a former assistant attorney general known for his aggressive enforcement of the Sherman Act, had been quick to sense that the old man might be induced to express a philosophy of economic laissez-faire so extreme as to bring ridicule on the whole banking community, and he pressed his final questions with an air of assumed respectfulness that led his witness deep into the trap.

"To a banker of your vast experience, Mr. Dunbar, the

experiments of legislators less versed in economics must often be trying."

"Well, sir, you might say that politicians, like the poor, we have always with us."

"Just so. And no doubt in your time you have seen our elected well-wishers come up with some pretty strange ideas."

"I could a tale unfold!"

"Might it not then have been helpful to the nation, sir, if more of your fellow bankers had seen fit to seek seats in Congress to help in the drafting of regulatory legislation?"

"Only on the premise that such regulatory laws are needed."

"And they are not, sir?"

"No, sir, they are not. I believe in a free market."

"Absolutely free?"

"Absolutely free, sir."

"You believe the Congress should exercise no control whatever over our giant corporations?"

"I believe that control should remain where it still largely is: in the chief executive officers of our greater businesses and in the heads of the major banking institutions. Competition tends to eliminate the inept, and the vital importance of a gentleman's word in any market transaction weeds out the dishonest. Of course, you are going to find rascals in any walk of life, but that includes the Congress as well."

Florham grew bolder now. "But does that not place power in the hands of our magnates comparable to the power of the Congress?"

"And what of that, sir? Are they not more qualified?"

"Tell me, sir. Are you yourself not one of the financial leaders of the country?"

"That is not for me to say, Mr. Florham."

"But if you are — and let us suppose, for the purposes of this discussion, that you are the greatest of such — would you not have a power comparable to that of the president himself?"

"Granting your hypothesis, yes, sir, I should."

I groaned inwardly. I had a vision of what the newspapers would surely make of this. They would shout from coast to coast that Lees Dunbar deemed himself more powerful than Warren G. Harding. And wasn't it true that he *did* believe it, even if he had not said it in so many words? It was not so much that my hero had made himself into a sounding brass or a tinkling cymbal; anything could be forgiven the senescent. What split my heart was that I was now beginning to see that this streak of megalomania had always been there. I had been fighting off my suspicions for some time, but now my vision had been horridly cleared. The Dunbar on the stand was not so different from the one I had worshiped in my mother's salon. Had he not always harbored the illusion that he was running his little world, like Napoleon in Tolstoy's *War and Peace*, pulling the straps and cords in the back of his plunging carriage in the belief that he was making it go? What was Wall Street in the obsessed imagination of Lees Dunbar but a parade ground where regiments in close-order drill executed his barked commands of "Squads left!" and "Left by squadrons!"? And what was I but the dazzled child who had believed it all?

Mr. Dunbar did not long survive the congressional hearing or the embarrassing publicity that followed it, though the worst of the latter I was able to spare him. His last days were marked by delirium, and I hardly left his bedside. His ravings about a Brazilian rain forest made little sense to me until at last he gave this seeming cohesion to them:

"That company we had on the Amazon. Do you remem-

ber, George? We had to clear a great area for rubber farm-
ing. And then that crazy manager chucked the work. After
the men tried to kill him, do you remember? And how fast
the jungle filled it all in. In *weeks*, George! In just *weeks!*"

I supposed this was his way of expressing the futility of
trying to make any permanent clearing in the jungle of economic life and that the poor old boy was experiencing some
of the same sour disillusionment that I was facing. I attempted to console him, but he did not seem to hear me.
Soon after he became entirely incoherent. When at last his
heavy breathing ceased, and I contemplated that strangely
still body, I was seized with a wild despair. Marion, hearing
my cry in the next room, hurried in with the doctor. I shall
never forget the shocked look on her countenance as she
contemplated mine.

I can appreciate now that what had shocked her was not
my grief but its cause. How could a woman, brought up to
admire the strong and superior in the male sex, feel anything
but distaste for a man who sobbed over the death of an old
gentleman who was not even kin to him? And how could
such a man take up the scepter that old Dunbar had meant
for warlords? Hadn't I just proved myself inept?

With Lees Dunbar's death I seemed to have lost my purpose in life; I began even to wonder if I might not as well
have lost life itself. For three weeks I did not go to the office
at all. I stayed alone in the house in Old Westbury, leaving
Marion and her father to cope with the problems of the estate
of which he and I were executors. I wondered at times if my
depression would not congeal into a permanent state.

Marion telephoned every other day to see how I was
doing. Her attitude was that of a nurse to a child whose
illness might have been feigned; she showed a businesslike
concern, but little sympathy.

"I suppose you must be aware there are important questions to be decided in the firm. Do you really think it's wise to be away?"

Of course, she meant the question of succession. Marion's conscience required her to warn me. But I had a distinct sense that she was just as glad to have me where I was.

"I can always be reached by telephone."

"All right, George. If that's the way you want to play it."

Mr. Dunbar, even approaching senility, had retained the function as well as the title of managing partner. His replacement would now have to be proposed by a nominating committee on which I, as a likely successor, did not sit. The only other serious candidate was Hugh Norman, and everyone knew that Mr. Dunbar had given me his preference.

It was my embarrassed father-in-law who drove out to Long Island to inform me of the firm's choice.

"I needn't tell you, George, how esteemed you are by all your partners," he assured me, after several throat-clearings. "But there does seem to be a feeling that your talents do not include a taste for the petty details of day-to-day management. Why should they? We have partners who even like that sort of thing. You're too valuable to be wasted on questions of promotion and demotion, or hiring and firing, or whether the reception hall needs redecoration or should we put urinals in the old washrooms."

"In other words, I should stay in my ivory tower."

"Now, George, you mustn't take it that way. This is all very well meant. You can say your partners are greedy if you like. They want to squeeze the last drop out of what you're best at. Leave administration to Hugh Norman. Nothing's too petty for Hugh. He's that *rara avis* who can see both the forest and every damn tree in it."

It was thus I first learned that, without either my advice

or consent, Hugh Norman had been chosen to succeed Lees Dunbar as managing partner of the firm. John Leslie was too old, and I . . . well, it was obvious that the membership did not see in me the image they wished to present to the world. It was also obvious that Marion had conspired with her father to promote her lover ahead of her husband. But wasn't the lover more of a husband than I?

The crisis for me was simply that the elaborately wrought inner scaffolding on which I had gingerly positioned my entire emotional life had been swept away overnight by the roaring cataract of Hugh Norman. At dreary dawn I found myself forlornly stranded on the grey banks of his relentless river. Where now was the long envisaged role of the arbiter of Wall Street? Oh, no, not quite of Wall Street — I was never such a fool as to think I could attain that, though in dizzy dreams such a pinnacle might have seemed almost achievable. But I had certainly visualized myself in a position of power comparable to that of Lees Dunbar, though without his hallucinations of national dominance. I had seen myself, much more modestly, as the umpire of corporate conflict within my chosen bailiwick, as a man who could bring some degree of governance into the chaos of my immediate economic vicinity, who could impose the order of the balance sheet on clients of messy thinking and even messier emotions. All I had wanted was to create a little civilization in my own back yard.

But now! Now I was only the expert diagnostician of corporate ailments. My analyses would still be sought by my partners, but how they would use them was no longer my affair. They would, of course, be concerned only with profit. In other words, my firm would be just like all the others. Some would ask: had it not always been? Who cared about George Manville's dreams? Did anyone

even know about them? Whom had I ever told but the un-
listening Marion?

8 I had never liked Hugh Norman, even before
his affair with Marion. Not because he was
cold; I have never minded coldness. It was
more that I suspected he was at heart unscru-
pulous. Oh, he would do everything according to the rules,
yes. But if he should ever learn that a form of profitable
wrongdoing had become at least tolerated by the "better
sort," I had little doubt that he would engage in it. His
morals, so to speak, depended on his private poll of the
marketplace. Like a courtier of Henry VIII, as interpreted
by Holbein, he would nurse no ideals. His courage consisted
simply in his willingness to risk the headsman's ax in his
pursuit of power.

He and I had always got on well enough, outwardly anyway, and he probably assumed we would continue to. He
undoubtedly despised me as a cuckold, but this was not a
matter that much concerned him. He exactly appreciated my
value to the firm, and now he had the satisfaction of knowing
I was no longer a rival.

How long his contempt and my resentment would have
jogged along uneventfully together without the incident of
the "pool" for the cornering of a certain stock, I do not know,
but that changed everything. Hugh asked me to attend a
small gathering of bankers and brokers at his house in Old
Westbury one Sunday afternoon. It was not a firm matter,
and it was not my custom to go in for such games, but I had

no wish to offend him without good cause, so I went, to be polite.

It was three o'clock on a peerless June afternoon. Most of the dozen gentlemen gathered in that dark library, surrounded by English hunting prints and standard sets of unread classics, would have been on the golf course had not a sharper game attracted them. They had lunched with their host; brandy and whiskey glasses were on the tables, and the air was heavy with cigar smoke. Having walked over from my own place in the glorious air, I felt an immediate revulsion.

"Ah, George, good, we can start," my host greeted me. I declined both drink and weed a bit brusquely and took a seat in the corner. "I think you gentlemen will all agree that this is a very pretty little scheme. I miss my guess if even the great George isn't tempted."

He proceeded, without interruption, to outline his plan to corner the stock of a vulnerable food-store chain of whose precarious financing he had had a careful study made. It was a simple and classic scheme. A graduated purchase of the company's common stock would drive the market price to an unrealistic high, at which point the pool would dump its holdings, leaving a gullible public to pick up the pieces in the subsequent crash. It was the same old game played half a century before by Jim Fisk and Jay Gould except on a smaller and less market-threatening scale, a kind of gentlemen's cockfight, disastrous largely to gambling short sellers with whose welfare the loftier bankers and brokers had little concern. It was not my practice to take part in such ventures, but I had never expressed disapproval of them. I had followed the lead of that greatest of stoics, Marcus Aurelius, who deemed it his duty to attend the bloody but popular games at the Colosseum which even he was powerless to ban, but, seated in the imperial box, kept his eyes fixed on some learned scroll.

"How about it, George? Can we count you in?"

"I think I'll pass, thank you."

I received some surprised looks, even a couple of critical ones, and a general discussion began in which I took no part. But I was confused by my own unrest. Where was the emperor, calmly perusing a tract of Zeno while the gladiators dueled below? I should have been above it all instead of being angry. Was it my function to interfere with bread and circuses? No! But I didn't have to stay and listen. I rose.

"Gentlemen, I leave you to your little frolics."

Hugh followed me out of the room to the front door. "You won't play with us, George?" he asked in his usual quiet tone. But there was a hint of a rasp in it now.

"No, I find I have put away childish things. Particularly when the other children are playing such dirty pool."

"Dirty pool! It wasn't too dirty for your sacred Mr. Dunbar to play!"

"That's a lie! He never did!"

"Really, George, you're too naïve. This business of the one god being Lees Dunbar and Manville being his prophet has got to have an end. Dunbar himself didn't dare tell you all he was up to!"

I went on my way without another word, but fury and sickness ate at my heart.

That night Marion accosted me in my study, where I was sipping a strong but single predinner martini.

"Aggie Norman just called me. She said you were shockingly rude to Hugh this afternoon. They're both very upset. She thought you must have been feeling ill or perhaps had had some piece of bad news."

"No, I'm feeling fine. And the only bad news I've had is

that Hugh and his little gang are planning a vicious stock market raid. But the good news is that I've taken a resolution which has given me the greatest satisfaction. I intend never to set foot in Hugh Norman's house again. Seeing him in the office will be quite enough."

"George!" Marion looked aghast. "Hugh and Aggie are my closest friends!"

"Oh, you may go there as often as you like. My good resolutions apply only to myself."

"But what on earth has Hugh done to you?"

"Nothing to me. And nothing to anyone else that he hasn't done a dozen times before. It's simply that now at last I *see* him. And I find I don't like what I see."

"But that's crazy!"

"Will you kindly then allow a lunatic to finish his cocktail in peace? I have nothing more to say on the subject of Hugh Norman."

Marion left me at this, but the following day, finding me still adamant, she proposed — and I, after some musing, accepted — this practical compromise. She would continue to go to the Normans', attributing my absence to a need of evening hours for the composition of an economic thesis, and Hugh and Aggie would come to us only for larger parties where he and I need exchange only a few formalities.

To tell the truth, I was surprised at my own obstinacy in refusing to cross Hugh's threshold. I suppose it was my only way of expressing my hostility to everything he represented to me. Other than that, I had no recourse but in the dreamland of fantasized violence. But what a hotbed that was! I imagined myself as a fiery U.S. Attorney, brilliantly reinterpreting old cases and laws to criminalize his pools. I saw him abjectly pleading for mercy before a stern, gavel-wielding judge. I even saw . . . but a truce to this childishness. The only benefit I conceivably derived from my rage and helplessness may have been in a dim, dawning sense of what I still might accomplish with my wrecked life.

Some such glimmer, anyway, may have prompted me to come to better terms with Marion. After all, our absurd and unnatural design for living had been as much my doing as hers. I invited her to my study at cocktail time to discuss how our compromise was working.

"Don't you really think, Marion, that under the circumstances my distancing myself from Hugh may have made all our relationships easier? Not only his and mine, but yours and mine and even yours and his?"

She examined the back of her outstretched left hand as if she were appraising her ring. "You and I have never really discussed my relationship with Hugh."

"What would have been the point? Obviously, I have accepted it. It was quite clear to me, long before you took up with Hugh, that your heart had not died with Malcolm Dudley."

"I was an awful goose about that, George."

"But I *knew* you were. Not a goose, but deluded. I knew you'd get over him, and I took advantage of that. That's why I have no moral right to object to Hugh. As *your* friend. He need not, of course, be mine."

"That's really very handsome of you. And if at any time you want a friend, a lady friend I mean, you will find me equally understanding."

"Oh, I'm sure it might even be a relief to you. But I shan't be needing one."

"You don't ever have the needs of other men?"

"Let's put it that I'm neuter. That avoids odious speculations."

But Marion did not want even her husband-in-name-only to be that. "I'd rather put it that you're virtuous."

"Thank you, my dear. I accept the mask." In fact, I was

virgin to both sexes, as ascetic as a priest. But only in priests was this considered admirable. "Let me put something more serious to you. Isn't divorce the obvious solution to our bizarre situation? You married me to become the consort of the future sovereign of Dunbar Leslie. You overestimated my claim to the succession. Why not marry King Hugh?"

Marion's expression was fixed now as she concentrated on the problem. "Hugh and I have discussed that, and we had guessed you wouldn't stand in our way. But there are two compelling reasons against it. First, a double divorce under the circumstances, followed immediately by the marriage of a partner's wife to the senior partner, would damage the reputation of the firm. And secondly, Hugh and I could not bear to hurt Aggie Norman, who has been so wonderfully understanding about us."

"More so than I've been?"

"Oh, yes. Because I haven't been giving Hugh anything that you really wanted. And Aggie has wanted Hugh to have the kind of love she hasn't been able to give him since her illness. I can't take anything more from her than I already have. She must remain Mrs. Hugh Norman."

I wondered if this generosity did not spring more from Marion than from Hugh. But anyway I approved it. "Aggie has told me herself that the polio gravely damaged her heart. She doesn't believe she has long to live."

"All the more reason not to hurt her! And of course she might live for years. I sincerely hope she does. But that brings me — plunk — to a very, very delicate question. One that I've been wondering if I'd ever have the courage to ask you."

"You mean, how good is *my* health?"

"Oh, my God, no! For what do you take me? I'm sure you'll bury us all. And I shouldn't blame you if you did it with some satisfaction. No, what I was going to ask you . . ."

She paused. "Really, I wonder if I can."

"I think I'm beginning to guess. Marion, are you by any chance pregnant?"

"No!" she exclaimed excitedly. "But you're very warm. Thank you, George, now I think I *can* tell you. I want to bear Hugh's child. Only one, if it should be a boy. Or more, until a boy came. Call me crazy if you will, but I have this strange feeling that a son of Hugh's and mine would one day be head of the firm! Oh, I'm sure of it! Try to believe at least in my sincerity, George."

"I should think the boy would indeed have an excellent chance. Your father would probably leave him his entire interest in the firm, and with that, added to Hugh's, he'd have to be retarded not to go far."

"Oh, George, don't make mock of it, please."

"I'm entirely serious. You and Hugh, I assume, would be counting on me not to deny paternity."

"Would that be asking for the moon?" But she held up a quick hand to keep me from answering and hurried on in an almost breathless voice. "Please, George, listen to me carefully before you decide against it. I know it's a tricky business, but I'm sure we can work it out if we all agree. Hugh, like you, has never had much interest in children. He'd only be doing this for me. He's perfectly willing to have you be the putative father. He promises he'd never interfere or embarrass you with claims about the child. And I'd see that you're never troubled with it. Oh, if you will see me through this, George, I'll be your staunch ally! We haven't been very friendly since I fell in love with Hugh, but you will find there's a lot I can do to make your life pleasant and agreeable. You'll see!"

I got up and walked to the window. I found myself unex-
pectedly touched. There was always something rather noble
about Marion; she showed it even with her present proposition. And, really, why should I not oblige her in this? I had
been, like my father, a *mari complaisant*. Before that I had
been, at least in Marion's mother's eyes, a *fils complaisant*. It
seemed only logical that I should now become a *père complaisant*.

"So you've found love at last, Marion." I turned back to
face her. "And Hugh is really lovable?"

"I love him anyway."

"And he you?"

She paused. She was always honest! "Ah, don't ask too
many questions. He loves me as Hugh can love."

Could she have realized that this was the one way to save
my pride? No, she was not so subtle.

"Have your baby, Marion. I'll go along."

These things are always known, or at least suspected. We
four put on a very good act, but I fear nonetheless that at
least a faint odor, something *un peu malsain*, emanated from
our performance. Certainly Marion's mother sniffed us out.
And it was I, of course, who bore the brunt of her unspoken
contempt. If Aggie Norman could be considered generous
in her self-effacement, and Hugh romantic even in an adul-
terous part, and Marion at least forgivable for a gripping
passion, what word could mitigate the scorn that might be
justly heaped on my role?

Perhaps most confusing to the prying observer was the
genuine devotion I felt for John Leslie Manville, born ten
months after my fateful conversation with his mother. He
was an enchanting little boy full of smiles, and when he
stretched out his arms to me I hoped indeed that he might

one day occupy Mr. Dunbar's chair. I'm afraid that Marion found my fondness for the child somewhat embarrassing, even showing a lack of taste, but Hugh, cold fish that he was, did not seem in the least to care.

I spent much of my free time now aboard my sixty-foot motor yacht, the *Arctic Tern*, which gave me all the haven I needed from worldly distractions. Whenever I could, I would head out to the ocean, sitting contentedly on the bridge by my skipper, a pair of binoculars hanging from my neck, as satisfied with foul weather as with fair. I eschewed the new habit of fitting out these beautiful vessels with period furniture and master paintings. I insisted that mine be shipshape in every respect: nothing placed on the gleaming bulkheads but charts, and all chairs and divans upholstered in spotless white leather. Whiteness indeed was everywhere on board except in the shining mahogany of table legs, rail tops and instrument covers; it enhanced my sense of the nothing from which we come and to which we shall surely return. It was white that made my boat almost disappear against the alabaster of the horizon. Only at sea was I truly alone with my aloneness.

And what of my stoic hero? What would Marcus Aurelius have said? That I had borne too much? Been too much a stoic? But had he not looked the other way from Empress Faustina's notorious love affairs? Nor had he objected to the naming of Commodus as his heir, although he might with a clear conscience have denied paternity of that cruel and dissolute youth. John Leslie Manville, at least, appeared to be a promising child. No, I concluded that the great emperor would have sanctioned my stand.

9

What finally aroused me from what I might term the spiritual hibernation of these years was the lunatic market boom of 1929. If my social relations with my fellow men had almost ceased, the activity of my mind had not. Indeed, it had taken advantage of my solitude to be more active than ever. The excuse that Marion had used to explain my absence from the Norman soirées — namely, that I was working on some economic thesis — had become true. I *did* now spend my evenings, as well as a good part of my days, in the office studying market trends, past and present, and seeking to determine what principles, if any, guided them. My goal was to place a finger on the very pulse of free trade. Were the rules which Mr. Dunbar and I had sought to apply to a tiny fraction of the general market extendable in any way to the whole? He had had a dream of accomplishing this by himself, but it had been the dream, at least in his senescence, of a megalomaniac.

It was perfectly evident to me, by the spring of that fateful year, that stocks had reached prices which could not be maintained. I was later to be deemed a great prophet, but in fact there had been many men of equal perspicacity. I adjusted my own portfolio to my dour prognostications, investing it in government obligations and the soundest blue chips, but I was much concerned with the firm's capital in which I, both as a partner and as co-trustee with Marion of her trusts, had a substantial interest. Hugh, who was primarily in charge of the Dunbar Leslie funds, was an all-out bull.

When I went to his office to discuss this, he pooh-poohed my doubts.

"Do what you want with your own, George, but don't fuss about the firm's. What he have, and what we're *going* to have, should make us more a power in the land than we've ever been."

"But you see, I don't believe that. Are you prepared to buy me out?"

He frowned. "Well, if you insist. Though it's a bit awkward, with everything invested right up to the hilt. I suppose we *could* raise the cash."

"And for Marion, too."

"Marion! Does Marion want out?"

"I haven't asked her. But I think she will when she hears my reasons."

"Marion doesn't know anything about the market, for Pete's sake!"

"She can learn. I owe it to her to safeguard her fortune. And that of our son."

"*Your* son?" Hugh peered at me with squinty eyes.

"Our son," I repeated firmly. "John Leslie Manville."

"Oh." He might have been reflecting that my reclusive life had affected my reason. "I see. Of course. Well, talk to Marion if you think you must. But I should warn you that I intend to talk to her, too. With sums like this involved, it becomes a serious firm matter. And Marion has always put the firm first."

"A New York heiress never puts anything ahead of what has made her that" was my parting shot.

I had been able to persuade two other major partners of the peril to the firm's portfolio, and I surmised that, if I could add Marion's voice to theirs and mine, Hugh might be forced to some compromise.

With this in mind, I approached Marion that same evening. She was home for a change, and after dinner, in the library, I outlined my plan. She only half listened until it broke upon her what it entailed.

"You mean you and I would join forces *against* Hugh?"

Life in this period had been perplexing for Marion. She had begun to put on weight, and this, with her increased social activity that now extended well beyond the firm (she was the queen of the charity ball), had probably diminished her interest, or at least her dependence, on romance. I had heard rumors in the office that Hugh had a lady friend from a very different social zone, and I had made it my business (always prepared) to verify this. I did not know whether or not Marion was aware of the affair, but if she had her suspicions, I wondered if a person as honest as she basically was might not have questioned her own continued right to call her lover to account.

"Does your loyalty to Hugh require you to place your fortune at risk?"

"But how can I be sure that it is? How can I know which of you two is right?"

"You can't. You may have to toss a coin. At least that would give you a fifty-fifty chance of not going down the drain with Hugh."

"Oh, George, don't be horrid! Explain it all to me!"

"I can't turn you into an economist overnight, my dear. You'll have to play your hunch."

"Can't you do *something* to help me?"

"I can do this. I can at least try to persuade you that honor doesn't call you to be more loyal to Hugh than he is to you." I handed her a card on which was typed a name, address and telephone number. "This is where you can reach Mrs. Ella Lane. I doubt that she will have an interest in refusing you any information you request. Her liaison with Hugh is well known in the social circles in which she moves."

Poor Marion held the card away from her as if it emitted a bad odor. "Why are you doing this to me, George?"

"I've told you why."

Her eyes slowly filled with tears. "I've known there was someone. But I didn't want to know who. Are you sure you're not doing this because you hate me?"

"I don't hate you in the least. I'm very fond of you, and I always have been. I'm doing this for you. *And* for your son."

She was silent for a minute. "Let me go upstairs now. I'll let you know in the morning what I decide."

At breakfast Marion's maid came down to deliver me a note from her mistress which simply read: "Go ahead with your plan." That morning I was able to induce Hugh to agree to reinvest in safer securities one half of the firm's capital. Thus are the major events of history often brought about.

When the great crash came that fall, Dunbar Leslie lost only fifty percent of its principal and escaped what might have otherwise been a receivership. My status in the firm was enormously enhanced, and a much humbled Hugh at partnership lunches was now careful to seat me at his right and to consult me on every question of importance. I never said "I told you so." There was no need.

Marion was much bewildered by these events. The re-emergence of her husband from, so to speak, the back chambers of the firm, whither he had been relegated by the wisdom of the old guard, seemed to defy the rules of the game as she had learned them. True, she had originally picked me as her candidate for the first spot, but had she not been proved wrong by her father and lover? And now here was the old struggle all over again! I was amused by her quandary, likening her in my mind to a sea lioness basking on a rock until the victor of two battling bulls should flop over to claim her.

Except she wasn't basking. She was making cautious overtures to me suggesting that we had drifted too far apart and perhaps should do more things together again. She even asked me if I would join her at the table which the firm had taken at the Waldorf-Astoria ballroom for a dinner honoring the secretary of the treasury. I firmly declined.

"In the first place, there's nothing to honor. Neither the secretary nor any of his party has done a thing to ameliorate the national disaster. In the second, I wouldn't be seen dead at a hotel banquet. We have established our pragmatic sanction, my dear Marion. Let us abide by it."

This may sound cruel. Marion was having her troubles. I knew that Hugh's Mrs. Lane had abandoned him for a corporate tycoon too great to be openly resented and that he was doing his best to reinstate himself in Marion's good graces. I was probably thrusting her back in his arms. But I didn't care. I had no further interest in the politics of the firm, or who was senior partner, and, having lived my life without the complications of sexual involvement, I had little patience for the heartaches and jealousies of people obsessed with their own genitalia and what to do or not to do with them.

Actually, I was probably helping Marion. She did patch things up with Hugh, and this may have been the best thing she could have done with her emotional life, or what was left of it. He probably continued to divert himself on the sly, but if he did, he took greater pains to conceal it. And in a year's time he had already started to take some of the credit, at least with the younger partners, for the investment policy which had saved the firm. The fact that I never bothered to contradict him lent credence to his claim, and by 1933 he was as strongly in the saddle as if his wisdom and leadership had never been questioned.

I have been accused of enjoying the Depression. There is some truth in that. I did not enjoy, certainly, the human suffering entailed, although I have never much concerned myself with human misery that I was powerless to allay. Pain and agony beyond my reach, at home or abroad or even on other planets, in the past, present or future — how could my sentimental wails mend matters? What I did enjoy was the interest of watching a national catastrophe unfold in very much the fashion I had foreseen, with the added excitement of feeling that the same mind which had seen it coming might offer some small clue in the problem of preventing its repetition.

For the years which followed the crash, bringing no return of our fevered prosperity, but, on the contrary, revealing even darker abysses, had begun to open up to many persons, like myself, the vision of radical changes in the management of our securities markets. The time might have come not merely to say "I told you so" to Hugh Norman but to add: "And here is what I'm *going* to tell you!" My life might not, after all, be a failure. There might still be a way to find consistency and even purpose in the career which had started in my mother's salon, discussing the Medici with its principal ornament, and had seemed to end with my relegation from the status of second partner to that of a mere economic consultant.

I had been working, off and on for two years, on a short text about the need for government regulation of the issuance and marketing of stocks and bonds. It had had its origin in my indignation at Hugh's little pool games. But now, with the new confidence engendered by my role in the firm's survival, I decided to expand it into a full-length book and offer it for publication. What I had once conceived as the policing role of the banking community I now realized had to become one of the many functions of Uncle Sam.

Principles of Market Regulation was published in 1932. It was read only by a small public, but that public was precisely the audience I had wished to reach: those economists who hoped to assist the new government if Hoover should be defeated and the banking world of downtown New York. The former hailed me; the latter decried me as a false prophet and, worse, a false friend.

Marion was thoroughly bewildered. She had tried to read my book and hadn't been able to make head or tail of it. But she had talked to her mentor.

"Hugh says you're trying to undermine the whole capitalist system!"

"On the contrary, I'm trying to save it."

"No one in the firm seems to think that."

"Have any of them any better ideas?"

"I don't know. It's all beyond me. I wish my father were alive to talk to you."

"Who knows? He might have agreed with me."

But it was only too clear, in any division between the firm and myself, which side Marion would be on. She was a tribal creature, and if necessary she would carry even the severed head of her spouse to the real chief. She had offered me my chance to be that, first in marrying me, then, when Mr. Dunbar had died, in trying to rouse me from my apathy, and, more lately, in offering me the resumption of a kind of partnership marriage, and I had failed her, and Hugh was king. But I was free of all this. I had my new thing. Detached, superior, in my box of observation, I could watch the inevitable unfolding of the drama below.

Marion's real trial came the following year, after the change of administration in Washington, when I was invited to go down to the capital and help with the drafting of the bill which was to become the Securities Act of 1933. This was the law which, more than any other, would open up the real struggle between right and left. My firm's executive committee came in a body to my office to beg me not to associate the name of Dunbar Leslie with such radical legislation, and when I calmly and politely declined even to debate the matter with them and requested them to leave me in peace, they departed in high dudgeon, but later delegated Hugh to appeal to Marion to intercede with me.

I was thus prepared on the night that she made her dramatic appearance at my study door, more than ever the Roman matron. Dressed for the reception at the Metropolitan Museum of Art whither she was bound, accompanied by the again faithful Hugh, to the opening of an exhibit of Hindu art sponsored by the firm, she was arrayed in red velvet with a necklace of large emeralds, and her fine auburn hair was for once neatly combed and set. Her full figure, erect in the doorway, was almost imperial in its static pose, and across her breast she was wearing the blue ribbon of a pompous Indian decoration which I had privately and ribaldly dubbed "the Order of Chastity, second class."

"I suppose it's true?" she began in a sad, lofty tone.

"Oh, Marion, sit down and have a drink. I'll tell you all about it."

"I don't care to sit, thank you. It's true, then, that you are going to betray the firm to which you owe everything and the class to which you have aspired."

"Aspired? My family was quite as good as yours, Marion."

"I am not speaking of blood. I am speaking of accomplishment and responsibility. Your father was a nobody. And we know too well what your mother was."

"Very much what you are, wasn't she?"

Marion looked more surprised than indignant. Her imagination was not capable of equating her relationship with Hugh, which she probably saw as a mating of gods on Olympus, with the humbler copulations of my mother and Mr. Dunbar.

"Your parents, I meant, were not leaders of the financial community. Which may explain why you have so little sense of loyalty. But have you stopped to consider in what light the captain of a great ship in a storm must view the man who jumps overboard to join the wreckers flashing a false beacon on the rocks?"

Really, Marion was magnificent. She must have written that out on her dressing table before coming down. But my amusement subsided when I recalled how much she resembled the aging Lees Dunbar before the congressional committee. None of those she called our financial leaders, or even the wives who had no real part in the game, were able to play it without waving banners and chanting martial songs. My momentary pity for Marion vanished when I considered that nothing would ever convince her that her values might be false.

"My dear, you are to Wall Street what Julia Ward Howe was to the Union. And your eyes will never admit that they have seen the glory of the going of the Lord. What I'm doing will no doubt raise the hackles of the old guard. I'm sure I shall be called some very nasty names. But not everyone feels that way. Even in the office some of the younger men think I'm doing a very interesting thing."

"I'm sure you're very persuasive. No one's ever doubted that. But Hugh questions whether our John, after this, will be accepted at Groton."

I laughed in sheer surprise. "But President Roosevelt went to Groton!"

"And the school is not proud of it, I'm told."

"Really, Marion, you and Hugh are being too absurd. Even the stuffiest people aren't going to hold what I do against a child. The boy may have to suffer a few cracks, but if he's worth his salt, he'll crack right back."

"Not everyone has your independence, George. Not everyone could take so lightly the bitter feelings that you have aroused."

"Lightly! I *welcome* the resentment of people like that! It actually exhilarates me."

This was too much. Marion seemed now to reach for a hidden weapon she had so far been reluctant to use. "Do you know what Hugh says your real motive is?"

"Oh, do tell me! I delight in Hugh's theories."

"He says you've always hated our world. That you've been biding your time for the chance to bring it down in ruins about our ears."

"And to what, pray, does he attribute this fervid rancor?"

"To your lifelong resentment of what Mr. Dunbar did to your mother! Nothing less than the destruction of his entire life work would make up to you for that humiliation!"

"I *see*. It's not unclever. For Hugh. But what about himself? Might not his reckless investment policies have concealed an inner drive to bankrupt the firm?"

Marion stared. "But what would have been his motive?"

"Ah, the id, my dear, the id. Who can penetrate its murky depths? But no, I shan't press that theory too far. And as to his of me, well, it might be as true as heaven or as false as hell. I don't think I really care. What difference do motives make? If they're unconscious, they're beyond our control. And even if they're conscious, are they our true motives?" I smiled in pleasure at the liberating idea. "Isn't there always a me-me-me behind the fair face of the do-gooder?"

"Is *that* what you think you are, a do-gooder?"

"Well, there you are, my dear. I do. Skip the gold stars.

Skip the demerits and black marks. Just look to the *effect* of what I do. If this new law will bring any kind of order to the marketplace, does it matter that I may be getting a jag out of kicking your old world in the teeth?"

"It should matter to *you*. It would degrade you."

"Let it degrade me, then. All that matters is the new law. Young John Leslie Manville may have a better Wall Street to work in. Even though he may have a few genes that will make him hanker for the old pirate days."

"George, please! That's a low one."

"Oh, Marion, you and I have been through too much not to be occasionally honest with each other. And anyway, we shan't be meeting too often, as I shall be moving to Washington. And when poor Aggie Norman dies — which can't be far off now — we'll get a quiet divorce, and you and Hugh can marry." I held up my hand to interrupt whatever comment she might have. "No, please, my dear, let's not discuss that. We both know it's always been in the cards. There'll be less scandal in that than in what everyone suspects now. And my heresy will ease whatever shock is left."

"Oh, George." Marion's voice was lower now, and she put her hand on a table as if to support herself. But she was always transparent. There was a deep gratification for her in my proposed solution. She could be sorry for George Manville and welcome the exclusion of this odd nonconformer from her life. "Will you let me help with the decoration of whatever house you take in Washington?"

"Oh, a hotel will do me. I have no idea how long I'll be there. And now you must get on to your party. But tell me one thing before you go. Do you remember the three categories into which your brother Bob used to divide his friends?"

"No. Why?"

"They had to be either swell guys, shits or genial shits. I'm wondering if I haven't at last qualified for the third category."

"What on earth are you talking about? I never heard such barnyard language!"

But I had no need to answer her. I was content. I felt fully the equal of all the Leslies and Dunbars and Normans now. And I was too proud to be proud of it.